W9-CFW-800

STORM RIDERS
THE NOVEL

A Tale of No Name

Author
Wing Shing Ma

Translator
Yun Zhao

Editors
Shawn Sanders
Kevin P. Croall

Production Artist
Anya Lin

US Cover Design
Anya Lin

Production Manager
Janice Chang

Art Director
Yuki Chung

Marketing
Nicole Curry

President
Robin Kuo

COMICS WORLD
www.comicsworld.com

English translation by
ComicsOne Corporation 2004

Publisher
ComicsOne Corp.
48531 Warm Springs Blvd., Suite 408
Fremont, CA 94539
www.ComicsOne.com

First Edition: April 2004
ISBN 1-58899-375-2

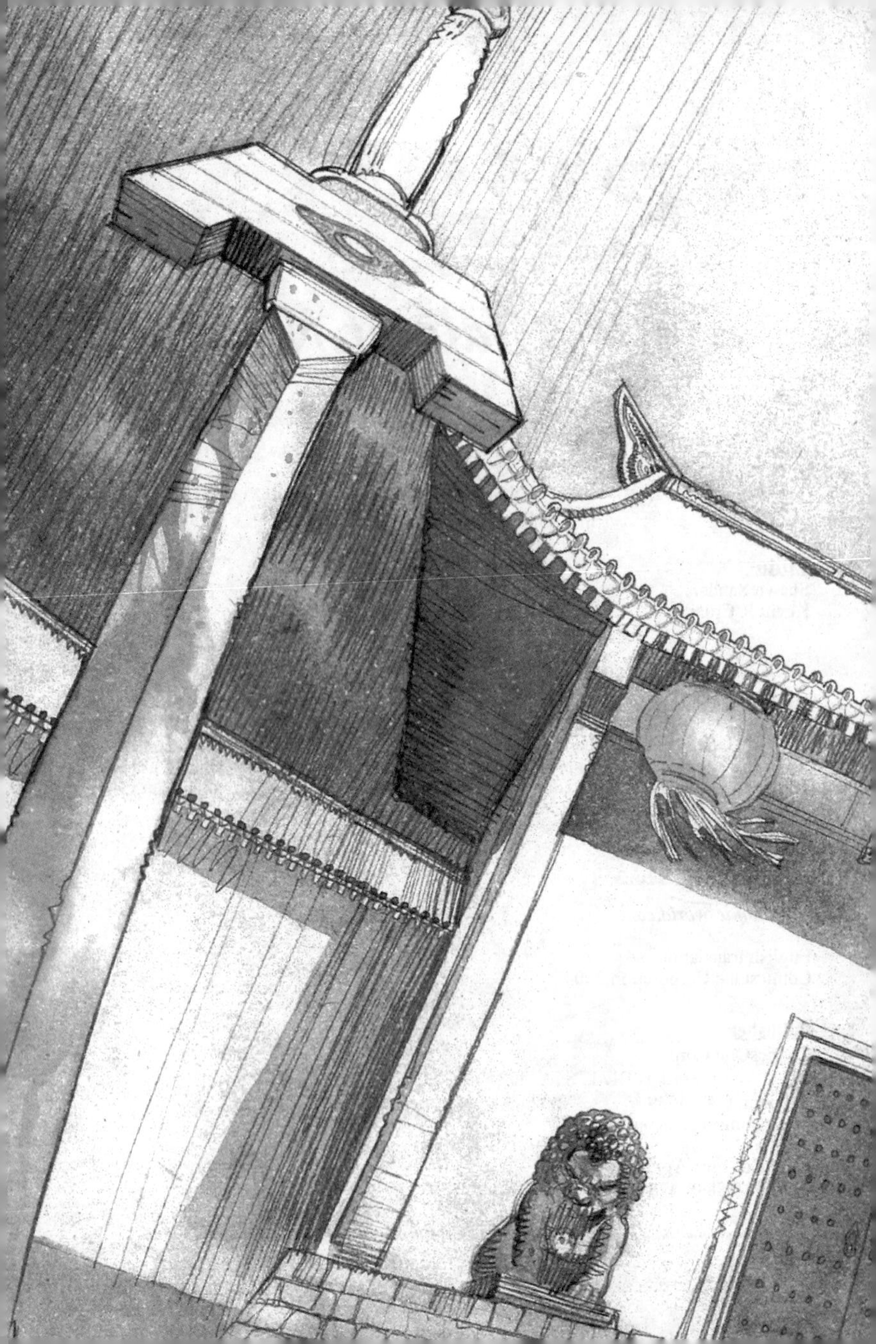

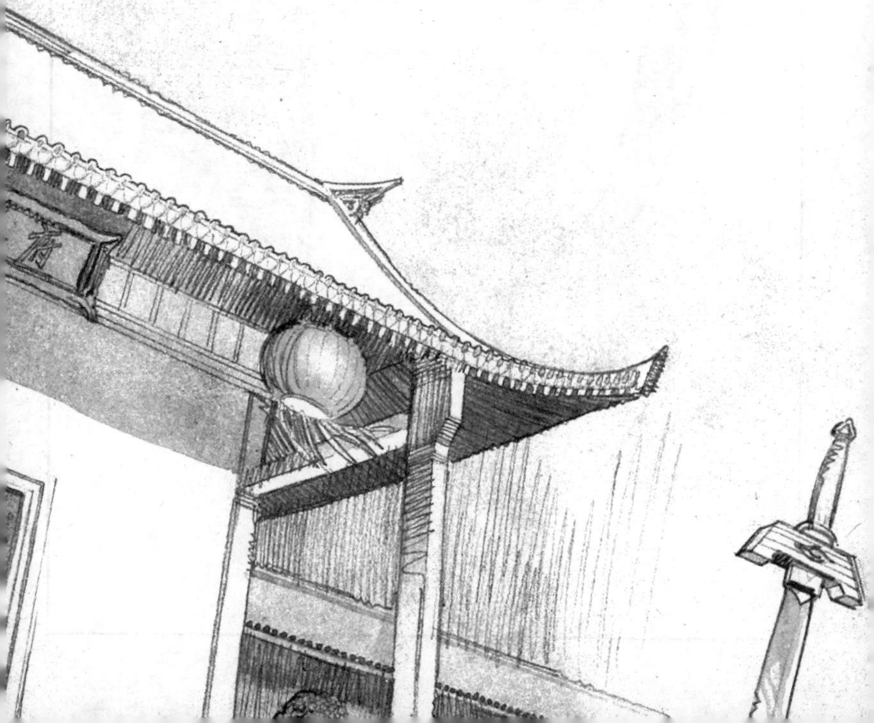

Nameless

Hiro*

*Hiro (Ying Xiong – Future/Should be Hero)
The name of this character has a phonetically similar pronunciation in Chinese with the words meaning Hero. When spoken aloud, there is no difference between the two. When written, the meaning varies only slightly.

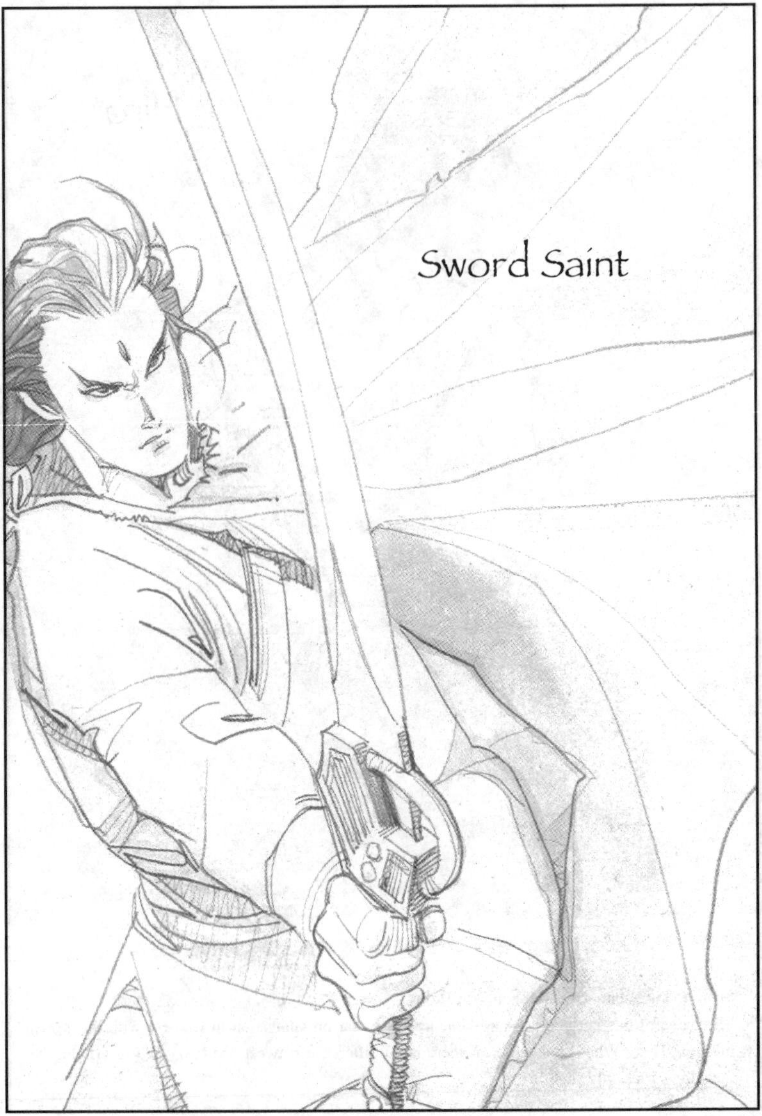
Sword Saint

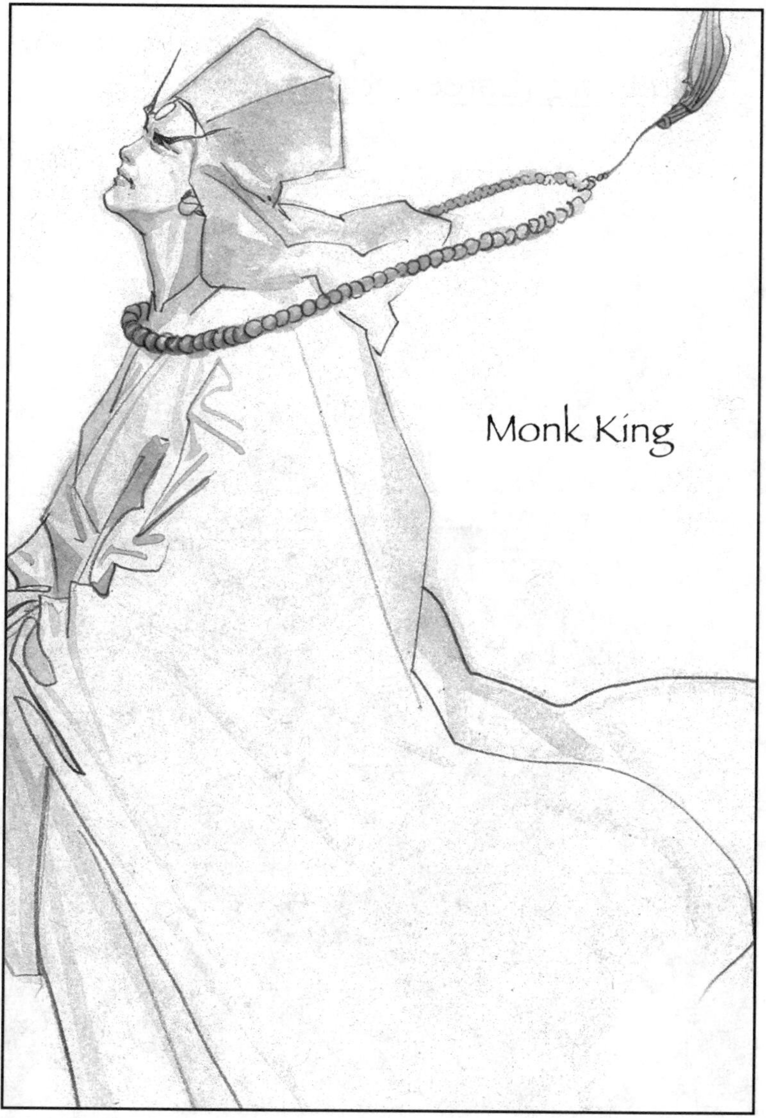
Monk King

Mu Long [Esteemed Dragon]

Xiao Yu [Little Happiness]

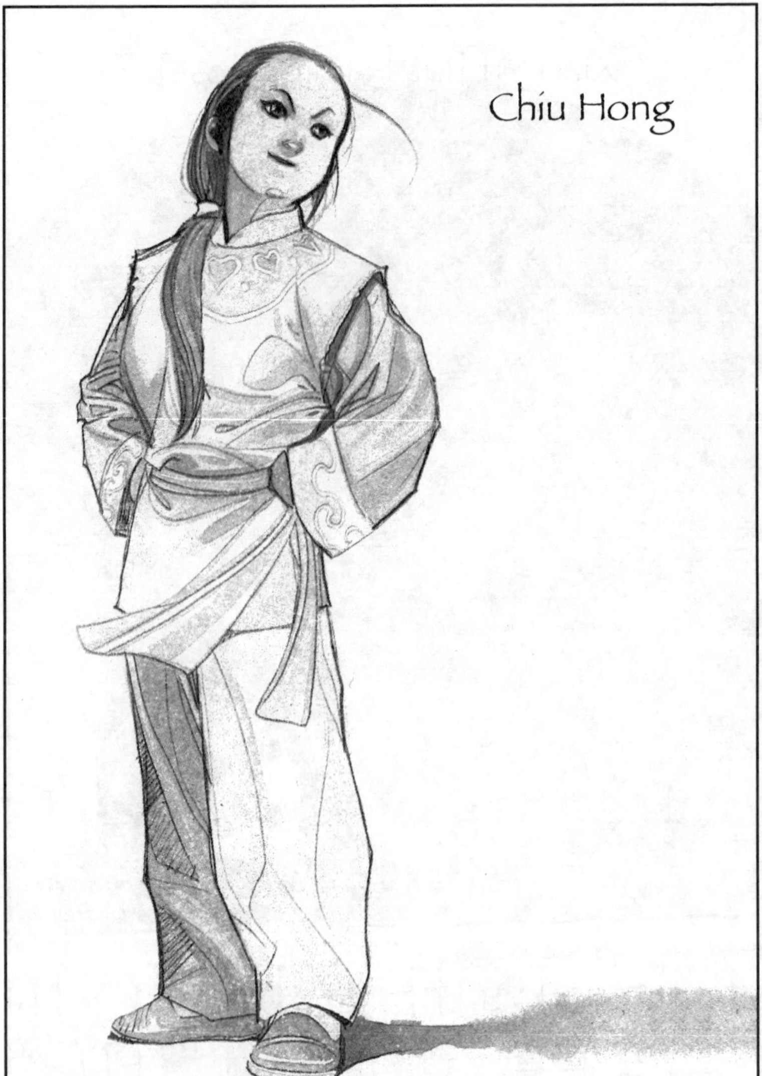
Chiu Hong

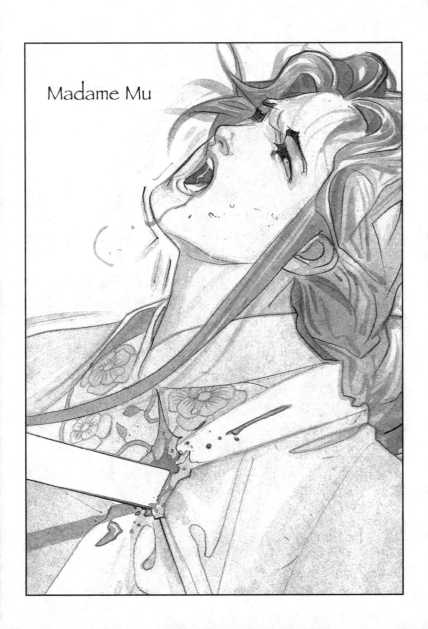

Madame Mu

Little Dragon King

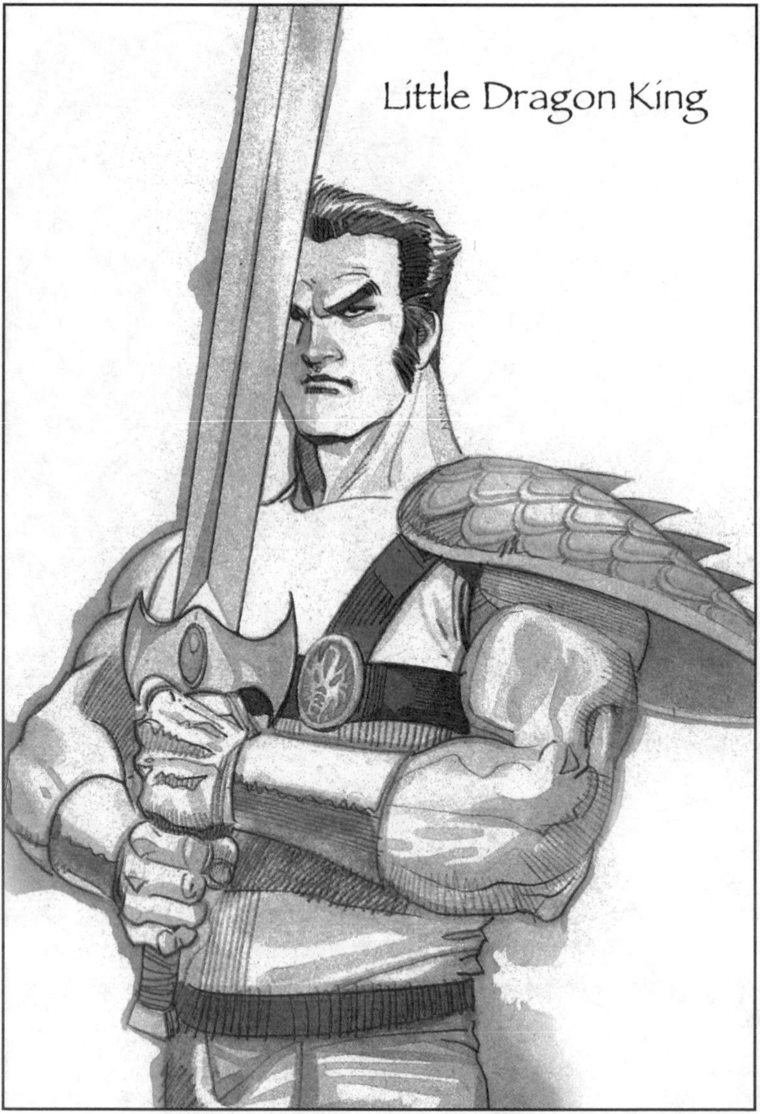

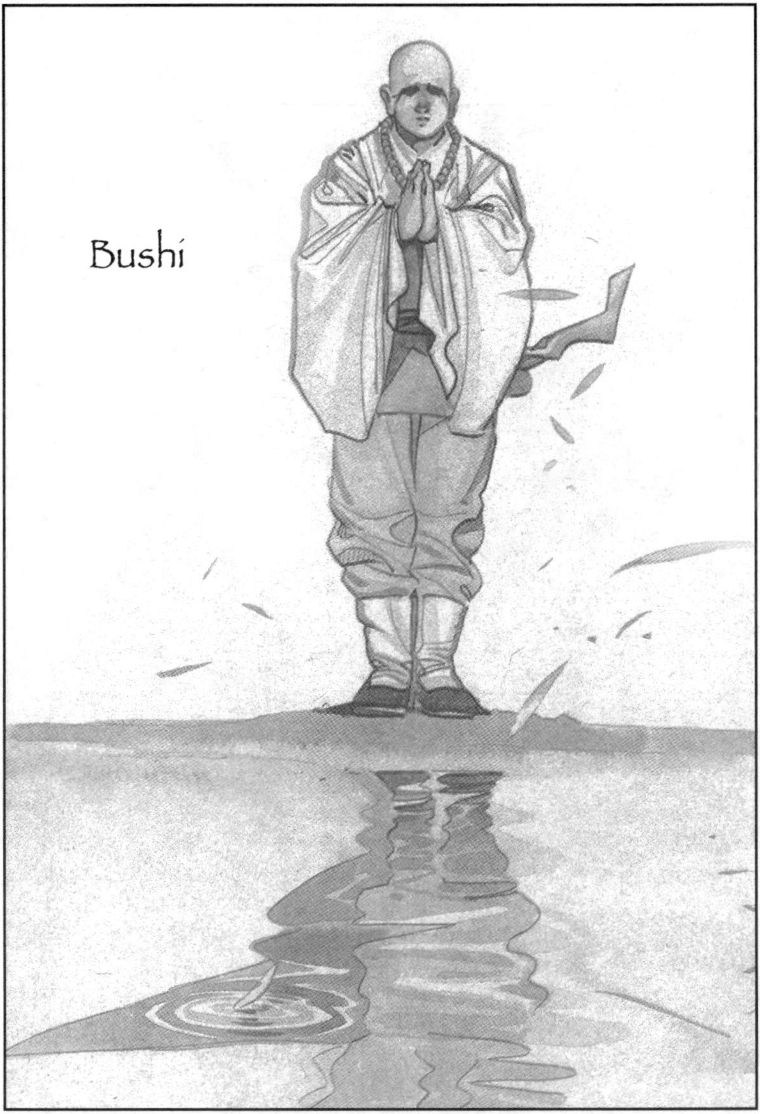
Bushi

Phoenix Dance

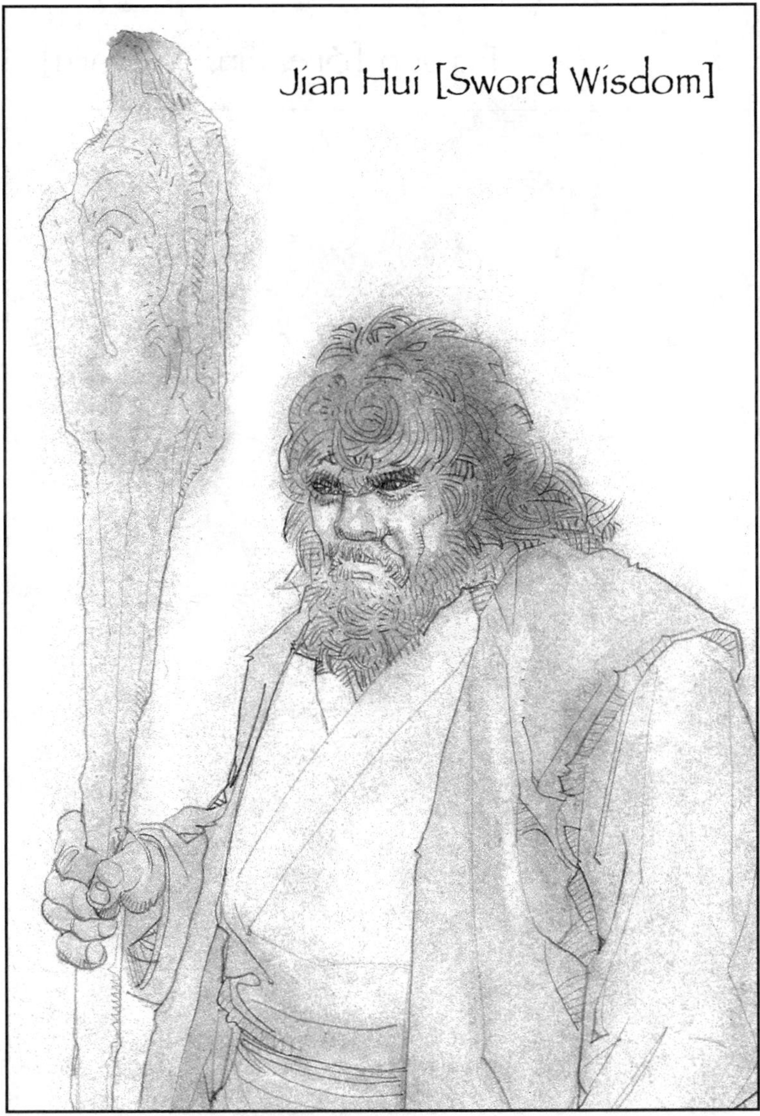

Jian Hui [Sword Wisdom]

Po Jun [Breaking Military]

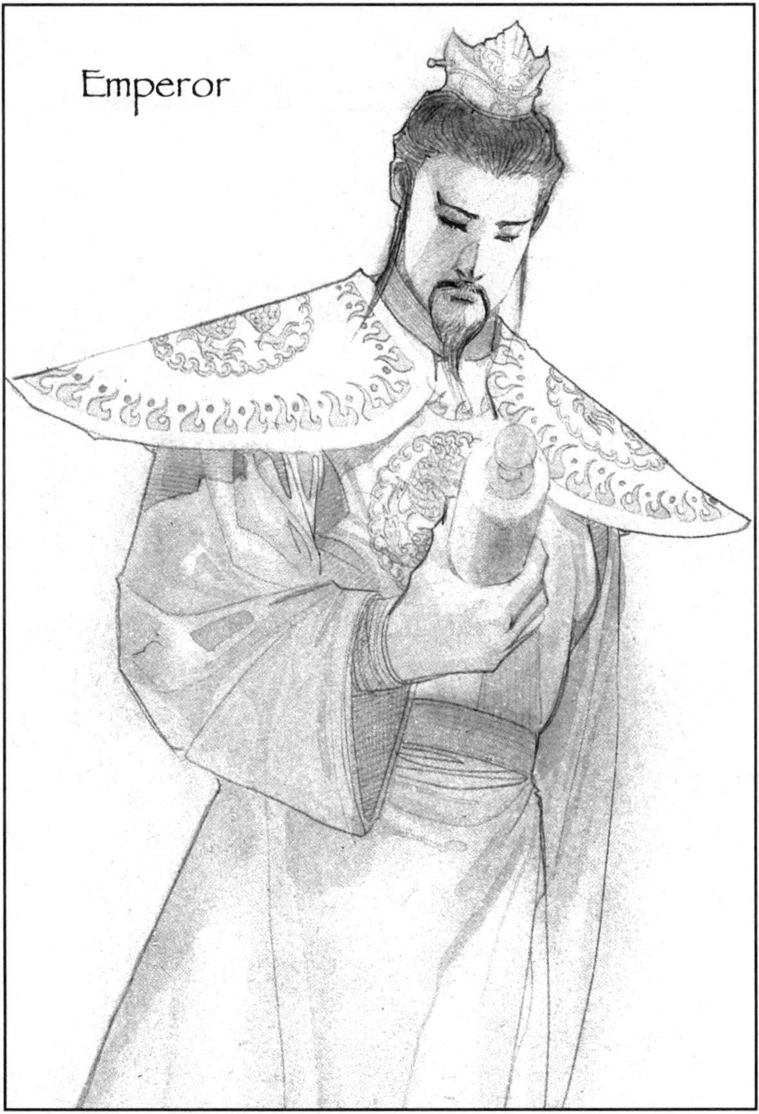
Emperor

Prologue

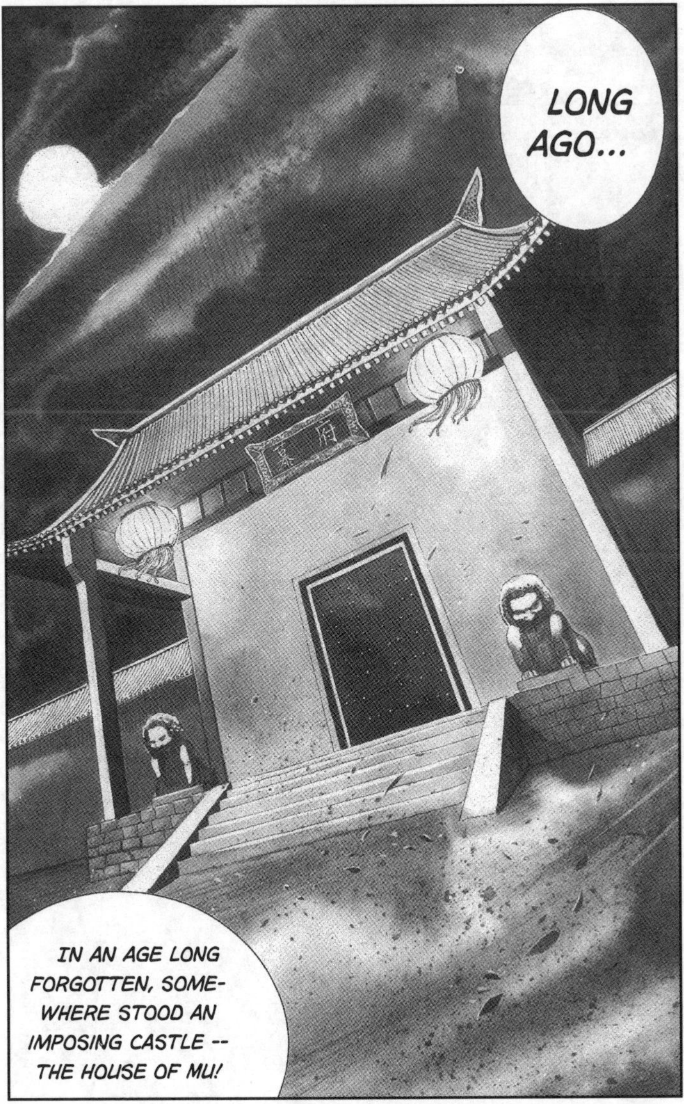
LONG AGO...
IN AN AGE LONG FORGOTTEN, SOME-WHERE STOOD AN IMPOSING CASTLE -- THE HOUSE OF MU!

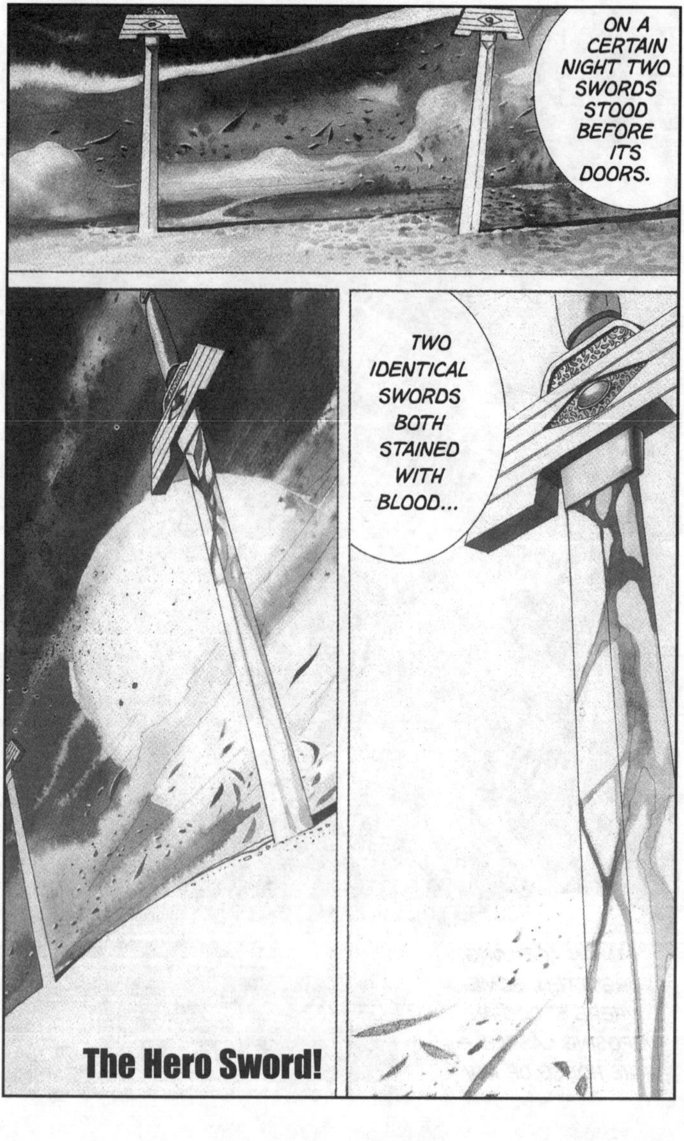
ON A CERTAIN NIGHT TWO SWORDS STOOD BEFORE ITS DOORS.
TWO IDENTICAL SWORDS BOTH STAINED WITH BLOOD...
The Hero Sword!

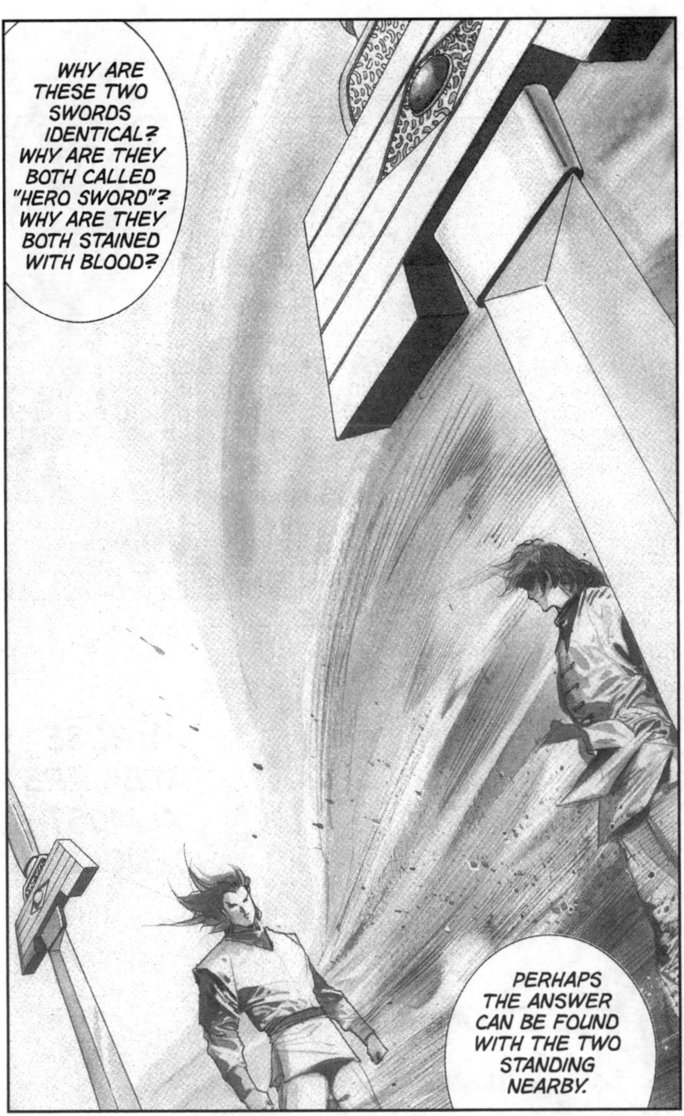
WHY ARE THESE TWO SWORDS IDENTICAL? WHY ARE THEY BOTH CALLED "HERO SWORD"? WHY ARE THEY BOTH STAINED WITH BLOOD?
PERHAPS THE ANSWER CAN BE FOUND WITH THE TWO STANDING NEARBY.

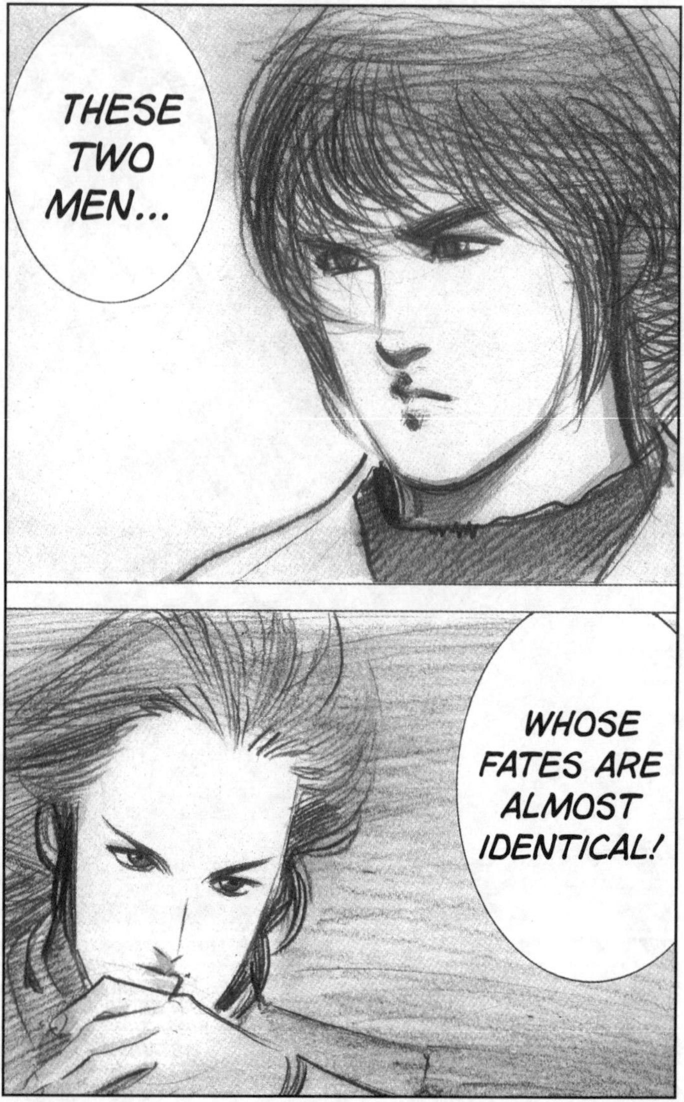
THESE TWO MEN...
WHOSE FATES ARE ALMOST IDENTICAL!

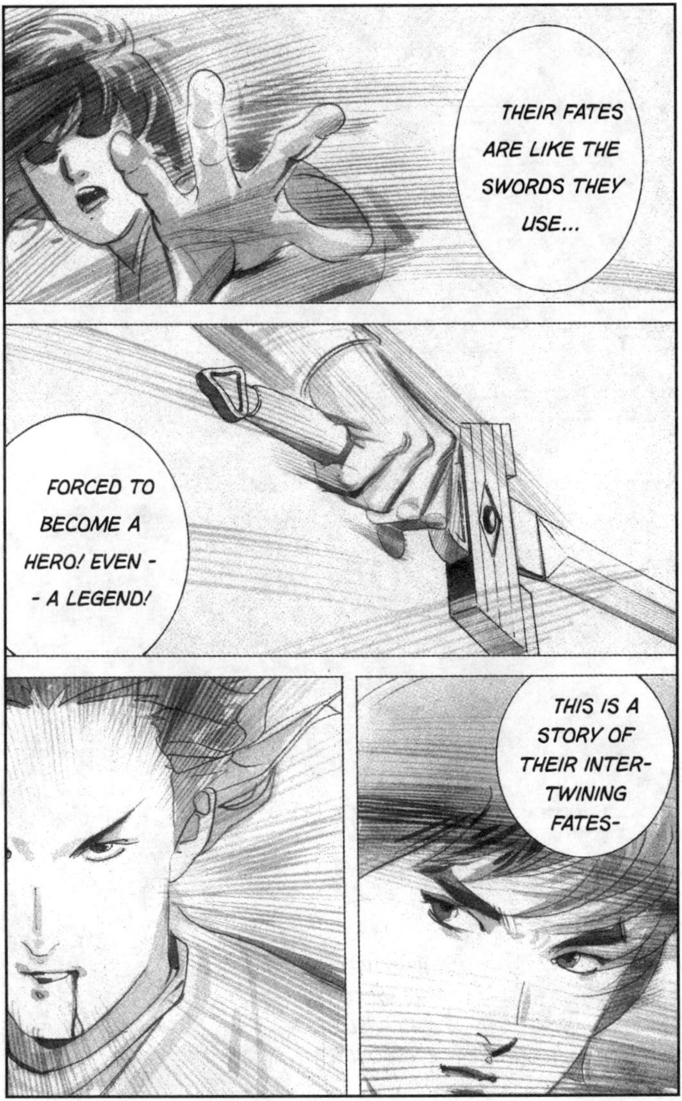
THEIR FATES ARE LIKE THE SWORDS THEY USE...
FORCED TO BECOME A HERO! EVEN - - A LEGEND!
THIS IS A STORY OF THEIR INTER-TWINING FATES-

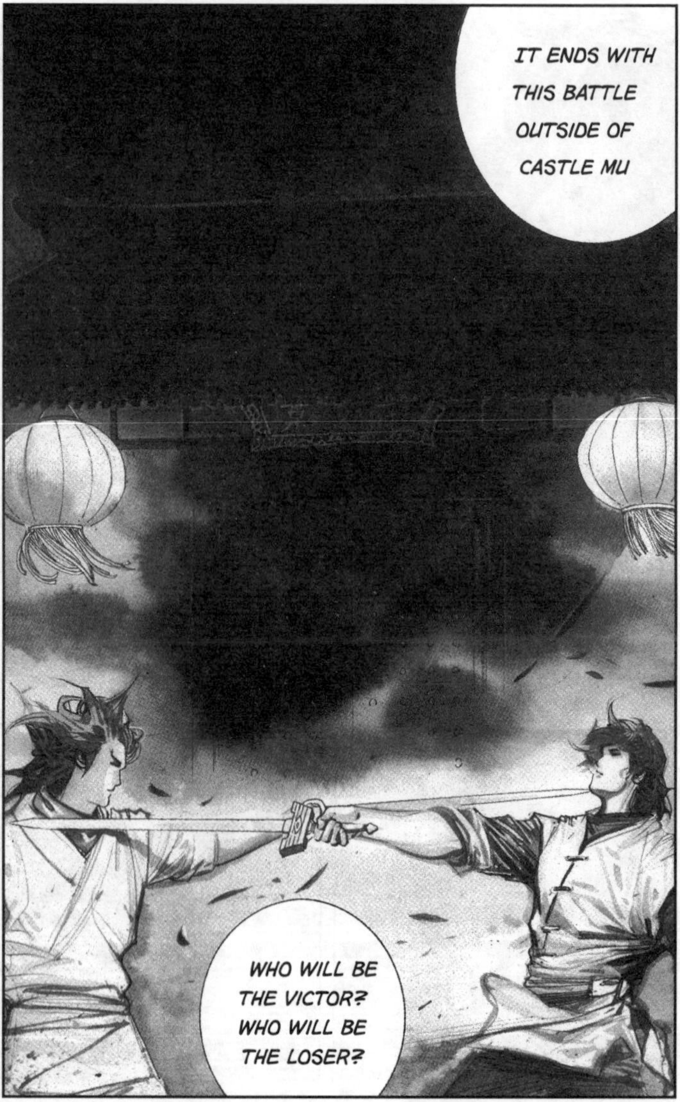
IT ENDS WITH THIS BATTLE OUTSIDE OF CASTLE MU
WHO WILL BE THE VICTOR? WHO WILL BE THE LOSER?

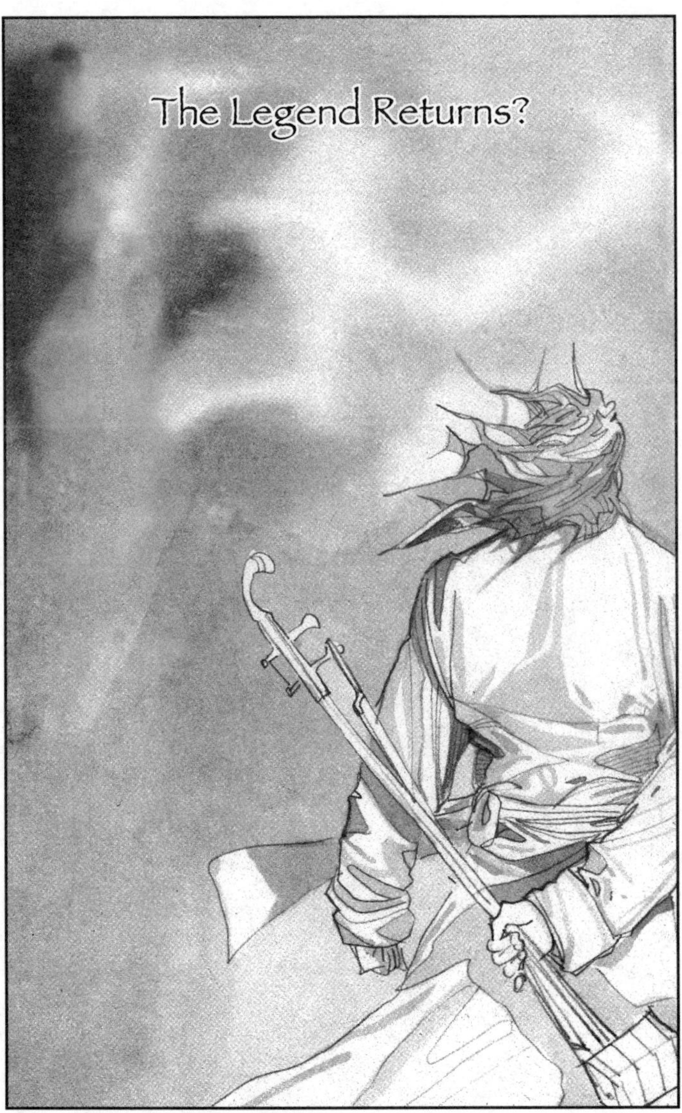
The Legend Returns?

Everything begins at the
World Fighting Association...

The World Fighting Association is an abyss for all love and hate.

Cloud, Wind, Kong Chi and Duan-Lang... After all the cycles, all the twists, all the turns and all the dangers, in the end, they always return to this place.

The World Fighting Association is also a tomb. A tomb for all lovers. Love does not flourish at The World Fighting Association, only combat. Those who fall in love are only digging their own graves. Like today, there are four people drawing ever-closer to that grave.

The names of these four are: Duan-Lang, Kong Chi, Wind, and someone not afraid of any tomb - "The God of Death," Cloud!

Yes! Cloud is like the dark death of a tomb!

It is this feeling Wind senses while traveling with him!

It's been five days and five nights; the World Fighting Association is a three-day travel. Wind calculates that even with the time it takes to return, there is still enough time to save Yorou.

Kong Chi is still unconscious inside the horse carriage. And Duan-Lang remains asleep from the "Heartless Potion."

He Carefully checks Kong Chi's pulse, making sure that she is still okay. Perhaps she has lived with the consciousness of "Black Iris" for too long. Once its presence has gone, she merely needs time to recover.

Duan-Lang is also fine. The Heartless Potion lasts only one month, after which Duan-Lang will be back to normal.

The person Wind is most worried about is… Cloud!

Cloud hasn't spoken to him in five days. On the outside he is like a fearful, silent tomb! Wind has traveled with Cloud before, and although Cloud is always cold and reticent, Wind usually manages to elicit at least a few simple responses.

Though the God of Death seems emotionless, there is a sense of envy: Cloud envies him because there is something Wind has that he will never possess--that smile of endless kindness! And Wind's tears.

But in these five days of traveling, even Wind's best efforts have failed to get Cloud to speak.

He is always staring forward, staring at the long road to the World Fighting Association. His face is like an iron mask, unchanged for days on end.

What reason lies behind Cloud's even more demure countenance? What has caused him to enter this tomb-like state? A tomb of the heart?

Wind had noticed Cloud's current disposition since Black Iris completed her life long wish of vengeance. Perhaps this mysterious brother with no background, no history, and no reason to be Conqueror's disciple had a similar tragic past that also demands vengeance?

Wind surmises that this is why Cloud has buried his heart in a tomb.

This is why he does not wish to speak to anyone, even Wind…

Wind dares not think further. He has long suspected since that incident in the West Lake, when Cloud changed from "Iron" back to the God of Death. Conqueror thought him already dead; there was no reason for Cloud to return to Conqueror's servitude. Yet he traversed that road without hesitation.

Also a proud and untamable God of Death would never willingly submit to Conqueror's will. Why does Cloud always return to do Conqueror's bidding? Is there something in the World Fighting Association? Something he desperately wants, such as…

The head of an enemy?

Wind shivered at the thought, and slowly looked at Cloud sitting by his side.

If Wind assumed correctly that Cloud was here for vengeance, then this Cloud, this God of Death, is ten times scarier than Black Iris. Though Black Iris has been long dead, the flame of her vengeance still burns on. Imagine the power of vengeance from the living Cloud!

He has a terrible nickname as the "Tearless God of Death" and he possesses fearsome martial arts, but...

...he is just one man!

Each man has his own weakness, pain and sorrow; though he must avenge an injustice that cannot be disclosed, he must silently endure this mission of vengeance. The pain that his heart suffers is much greater than Black Iris' whom is long dead!

At least Black Iris still had her master and followers who understood her pain...

Cloud endures the pain put upon him by others and in the end he remains silent without any word of complaint. This man must have a heart of iron. This man is truly fearful...

Admirable...

And pitiful.

Perhaps his melancholy is more severe than Wind's, whose father disappeared and mother abandoned him.

Wind didn't want to think on this any further. It was really not his place to pass judgement on Cloud's past or future motives. And so the two of them traveled silently.

Until...

Until twilight, when their horse-drawn carriage passed near a clear stream, and Cloud suddenly spurred his horse on!

Wind was perplexed, and urged his horse on to keep up with Cloud.

"Cloud..." he called. "We still have a way to go, why are you in such a hurry?"

Cloud did not reply, gazing intently at the clear river water, as if aware of something no one else could see.

Wind followed suit and looked to the river, but did not find anything of interest.

"Brother Cloud, what are you looking at?"

This time, the reticent Cloud finally spoke, though strangely...

"I'm looking at the aura of water!"

The aura of water? Even water holds an aura? Wind almost laughed. He thought Cloud must be getting really bored. But just at that instant, the laughter died in his throat as he felt....

An aura wafting in from the river!

A very special aura, one of a mysterious unknown martial arts master!

The aura of a legend!

God's have a unique aura, just as demons. In Wind and Cloud's journey among gods and demons, they have always felt that each gave a sense of superiority and overwhelming arrogance. Yet the aura exuding from the river water was like a mythical legend; exalted, yet humble, brave, yet wise. Everything was just right, not too hot and not too cold; a light, perfect legend.

Legends... they do not really exist.

Legends are the collective hopes and yearnings of the masses...

But the river water is clear; there is nothing beneath its waves, not even a single fish or shrimp... Where does this aura come from?

To his credit, Wind quickly figured out that the legendary aura was not coming from someone present, but rather from a pocket of residual chi left in the river!

A competent martial artist understands that everyone has their own unique "chi." Especially those who are well versed in the arts; one's chi is impossible to hide. But unbeknownst to most people, each life form has its own unique chi, even a simple blade of grass, or a flower, a rock, a puddle--each has its unique chi signature.

Thus, if someone possessing that "legendary" chi passed this river, and washed his face in the stream, then the water's chi would be imbued with that person's chi. Though the person is long gone, his chi lingers.

It's a testament to the strength and depth of his powers.

Of course, a normal person would not be able sense anything special about the water. Perhaps this chi might even slip by a good martial artist, but not to Wind and Cloud.

They both can detect the legendary aura left in the water--does that mean they are top martial artists? Does it take a God-like or demon-like skill to detect such a legendary chi?

Perhaps! Though they have just fought an arduous battle and have only half of their chi remains, it is still enough to rival the chi of the gods or demons.

Suddenly, the lake exploded with a loud booming sound! A pillar of water shot up high into the sky, spread like fireworks in midair, and then disintegrated like dissipating smoke.

How amazing! If this person merely washed his face in the river, and

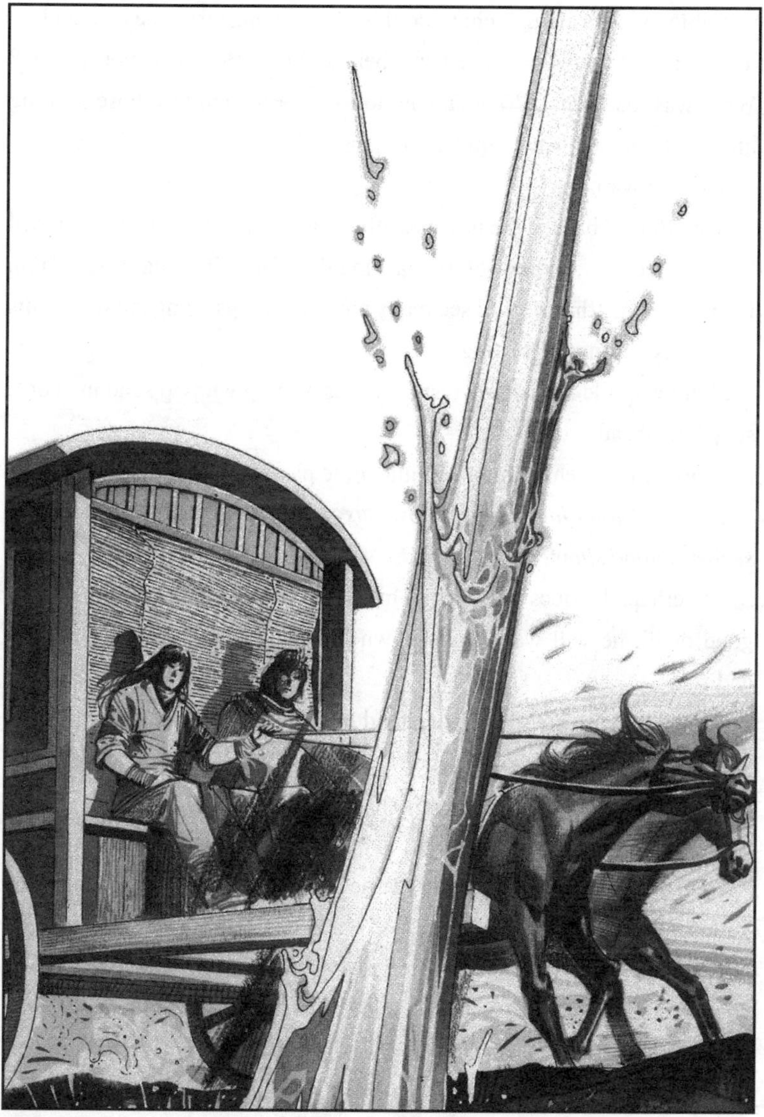

was able to leave enough chi to do this, then he must truly be a legendary martial artist! Yet, why did he leave behind this explosive demonstration? What was his purpose? Perhaps he left it as a warning to those seeking him, to desist and leave him be. Perhaps…

A gentle warning.

Wind looked back at the now peaceful waters, and said: "Cloud, we still have a three-day journey before reaching the World Fighting Association. I have a feeling that we will see many amazing things along the way. This journey is getting interesting…"

Cloud was silent, his only response was a sharp whip to send his horse speeding ahead!

Wind hurried behind him, a slight smile passing across his lips.

Because Cloud hurried to follow this path! Perhaps he's interested in seeing a good show?

Or perhaps he does not change his path for anyone or anything... For good or ill, he will walk alone down his path of destruction. Until the end…

Wind could not possibly understand the feeling in Cloud's heart! Cloud was anxious to see someone, but kept it to himself. Someone he hasn't seen in many years--a person he really wants to see.

The "uncle" in black clothes!

This is someone that forever earned Cloud's esteem when his was younger.

The most powerful and mysterious of all masters Cloud had ever encountered. The black-clothed uncle's incredible aura and his awesome powers remain forever etched in Cloud's mind. He is forever somber, mysterious, and, like a hero from a tragic tale, one that has vanished, but always ever-present…

Cloud knew that the legendary aura in the river water must have been left behind by the black-clothed uncle! He is the only one worthy of being called a legend!   And the only individual able to impress the God of Death. If young Cloud had not been forced to part ways with this uncle and continue on his path for vengeance, this legend would surely be Clouds most honored master! Regardless of their separated fate, he is still the one Cloud finds most worthy of admiration!

Cloud wants to see him, to let him know that the young boy he once helped is still alive! He wants the black-clothed uncle to know, not to belabor the righteousness of his path, that Cloud is still well!

Cloud knows the man's temperament. Even though he let Cloud go so many years ago, he will still worry and feel troubled over Cloud's future. So Cloud hurries to meet him, to let him know that the young boy he has worried about over so many years, has grown into a powerful young man.

Yet, the black-clothed uncle remains an elusive figure. Cloud and Wind did not detect anything further along the road.

Wind noticed a tiny crease on the brow of the usually cold and cool Cloud. Surprised, he asks: "Brother Cloud, it seems you're searching for something, something important to you? What might this be?"

Cloud did not immediately respond. After a moment, he slowly says: "I am looking for a Legend. A myth!"

Legend? Myth? Wind was stumped. And he wonders why is Cloud being so mysterious today, always speaking in riddles? He can't figure it out. Luckily Cloud's last words are the closest to a straight answer Wind has heard in quite some time. Usually when Cloud speaks, it is always with an icy tone, but this is the first time Wind has heard him speak with a flicker of emotion, as if he's searching for someone dear to him...

Who is this person worthy of remembrance by the God of Death?

Wind never knew of Cloud's past before he joined up with the World Fighting Association. He was curious and on the verge of asking, when...

Cloud scanned the weeds to the left of the horse carriage and spat out three words: "Something is wrong!"

Wind sensed the danger at the same time. Instantly he backflips onto the top of the horse carriage. His speed and agility earned the hard-won respect of Cloud. From his vantage point atop the carriage, Wind is able to see further than Cloud. Scrutinizing the area Cloud pointed out, Wind finds nothing out of order, as if the danger has disappeared, just a shabby teahouse lying about a hundred yards past the weeds.

Some are selling tea. And others are drinking tea.

If that danger Wind and Cloud sensed is real, then perhaps the cause of it is...

The teahouse.

Wind looked down at the imposing Cloud sitting calmly in the driver's seat.

"Brother Cloud," he begins with a warm and mischievous smile, "the journey has been long, shall we pause for some tea?"

Cloud and Wind tether the carriage outside the teahouse and proceed inside.

The interior was extremely sparse, even downright shabby. From first glance, the teahouse was in disrepair. The boss and the workers were all wearing mismatched clothing, and the tea was less than spectacular. Fortunately, most of the customers were road-worn travelling merchants, looking for a moment's rest, so the quality of the tea mattered little.

Wind and Cloud were not tea connoisseurs either, and when presented with two cups of plain tea, they sipped it without complaint.

After finishing, they remained seated, for they had discovered something.

That sense of danger! It's here!

Cloud and Wind's senses are incredibly honed. In unison they turn in the same direction and find four merchants sitting around a table. But not merchants, they are actually four martial artists disguised as travelling merchants.

The sense of danger emanates directly from them!

The four look to be about 40 years of age. They are all martial arts experts, and can control their chi at will. The sense of danger disappeared when they relaxed their chi. Currently, the four are on guard and sit taut as a tightly drawn bow string, their chi escaping along with their tension.

Who could be causing them this tension?

From the sense of danger their chi is emitting, it is clear that they intend to kill. But who?

Is the victim, perhaps… A Legend?

Wind and Cloud immediately grasped the situation, yet they made no motion to act. Wind uses his "Ice Heart" skill to listen to their whispered conversation.

"Second Brother, are you sure that 'he' is coming?"

"It's true! Big Brother's spies report that he comes to this teahouse everyday, rain or shine!"

"But Second Brother, I just don't understand; didn't he… die many years ago? How can he still be around? Besides, a famous warrior like him, why would he come to this god-forsaken place?"

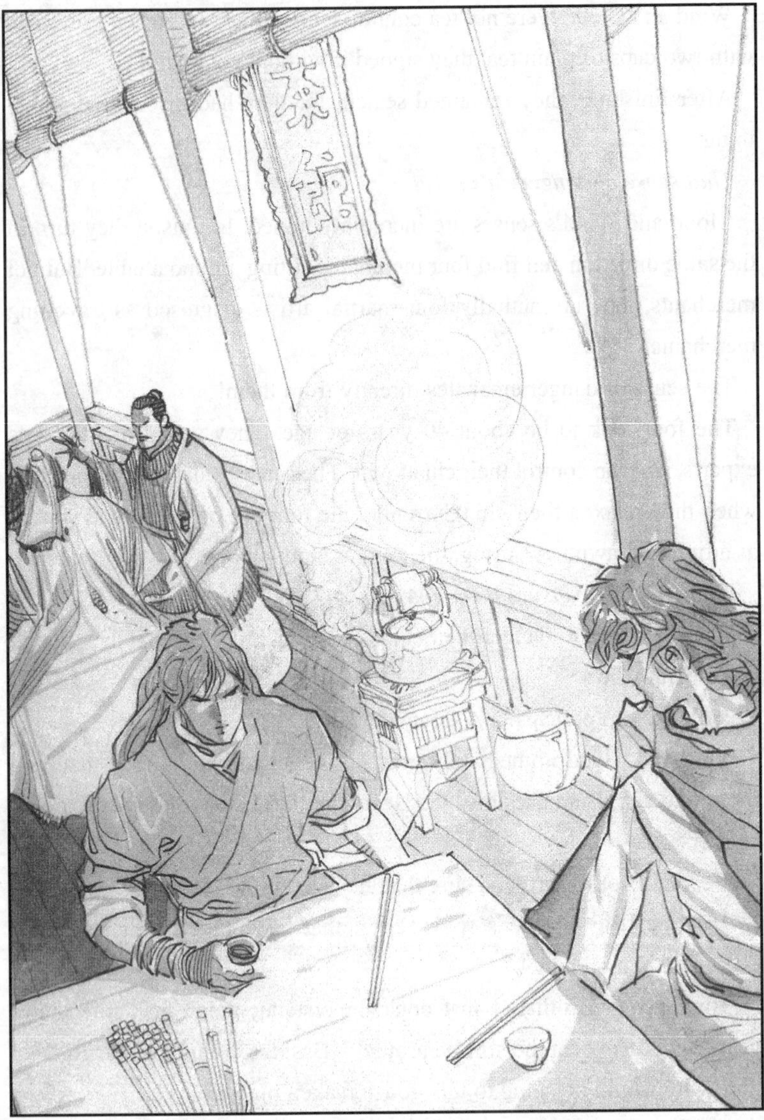
茶館

"3rd Brother, I think I can answer this question! How could such a legendary fighter die so easily? I'm sure he is just using the rumors of his death as a cover-up. Why is he hiding in this place? Why do many of the world's top fighters, for some reason, like to torture themselves by living in shabby conditions?"

"Fourth brother, you are right. Regardless of why he is hiding here, today we, the 'Four Gentlemen of Long Mountain' have found him. When he arrives, he will never escape our 'Gentlemen Array.'"

"Yeah, Big Brother is right! Remember how powerful he is. He single-handedly broke out of an attack by all ten notable schools. But times have changed. Even if our father wasn't a match for him, it doesn't mean we will not be able to best him! We created the 'Gentlemen Array' from our father's 'Gentlemen Sword' technique. It is many times more powerful than the original. I dare say it is the world's most powerful array; it will succeed! At last we will be able to avenge our father!"

So this is a story of revenge for a father! Although Wind heard it, he was not sure he agreed with them.

According to the four brothers' story, their father joined in a group attack and died as a result of an unsuccessful ambush; yet the conduct of the ten schools gathering together to attack a lone man seemed dishonorable. Wind felt that their father deserved his fate for taking part in such a despicable act.

What incredible power that one man must have possessed to repel the combined might of ten martial arts schools!

Wind thought of the two brothers from the "Wind Moon Clan" who relentlessly pursued Uncle "Ghost Tiger" seeking the whereabouts of his master. Wasn't Uncle Ghost Tiger's master supposedly this legend who thwarted the attack of 10 schools? Are they one and the same?

The shame left behind by the ten schools' failure seemed to have spawned numerous revenges.

Wind looked back to Cloud and found him deep in thought. Though Cloud did not possess Wind's Ice Heart ability, it seemed he still deciphered much from reading their lips.

The Third Brother spoke: "So Second Brother, what does that guy come to this shabby place to do?"

"Him? Hehe… Our spies told me that--and you won't believe this--he's here to…"

"Ah, speak of the devil, there he is!"

"He…"

"Is here!"

The Four Gentlemen of Long Mountain knew he was present, because they heard a voice coming in. Of course, Wind heard it as well and even Cloud noticed. Because that sound is not hard to identify, it is the sound of an erhu. The erhu is a traditional Chinese string instrument. There are two strings, with the bow inserted between them. With a range of around three octaves, it's sound is rather like the violin, but with a thinner tone. Usually the music of the erhu is associated with tragedy and sorrow. And the issuing was an extremely lonely and sorrow filled one!

It is difficult to imagine that anyone could play such a lonely and sorrowful melody on the strings. As if in all the world, he is alone, mournful for something sad and regrettable.

The lonely melody was sad enough to break the heart, as if loneliness had become a weapon to pierce one's soul… Though the sound was sad, Wind and Cloud did not feel melancholy, and instead were startled because they have heard it before!

When Wind was eleven, and living with Uncle Ghost Tiger by the snake caves, he heard the notes of this song with his Ice Heart Mantra. He's always felt since then that Ghost Tiger's Master might still live, yet he has never had the opportunity to meet this master.

Wind will never forget the wistful notes he heard through the snowstorm, a melody identical to this one.

How can this be? The melody of the erhu seems to be no ordinary local tune. It seems carefully arranged by a master artisan. It must be the same person that was playing on that winter day, could it be... that Ghost Tiger's Master is still alive?

That once formidable warrior, who had used death to hide from the world... What would he be like today?

Wind became more curious. He wanted to find out for himself, the master who inspired such loyalty in Ghost Tiger. Instantly, Wind was filled with anticipation and eagerness.

Wind's anticipation paled to the depth of Cloud's yearning. Because the sound of that erhu was a hundred times more vivid and familiar to Cloud. Cloud could never forget that time he spent with the black-clothed uncle so many years ago. How could he forget the Hero Sword that rejected him? And how could he forget the technique that he had secretly learned from that black-clothed uncle -- "Endless Pain?"

Even more unforgettable: the sound of the erhu playing every night...

That song, he heard it so many times. He could identify it within the first three notes! He knew that it must be the black-clothed uncle.

Only he could play something so vibrant, yet miserable!

Only he can outlast "forever"...

Beads of Sweat begin to form on the brows of the Four Gentlemen of Long Mountain; even Wind and Cloud were not immune. The person they've all been waiting for approaches.

At this point, all in the teahouse were attracted by the sound of the music, looking out toward the source, but when the musician appeared, the music stopped. A deep male voice carried across, wistfully sighing: "Speak of heroes, lament the would-be heroes, though their fates are similar, one is a hero the other would-be. They battle all their lives seeking only a calm life. Looking back, they find that their lives were never their own."

The music is filled with endless sorrow and regret. Cloud instantly recognized the voice of the black-clothed uncle.

"Is that really him?"

"But why would he come to this shabby teahouse? Isn't he in seclusion, refusing to see anyone?"

Cloud didn't have long to ponder, as a tall masculine shadow began walking towards the teahouse, followed by a sigh.

Seeing the man's shadow, the Four Gentlemen of Long Mountain gripped their swords tight. Wind was eager to meet this legendary figure.

Cloud's face was full of seriousness, not because he didn't want to see the black-clothed uncle, but he has in fact been eagerly waiting this moment.

There! Cloud could just barely make out the silhouette in the distance! He is just as he remembered. His hair carelessly tousled with a long plain-colored robe. He looks exactly the same as when Cloud met him so long ago.

He instills the same feeling of awe and respect as he use to. A hero worthy of worship and adoration.

This man, a mythical hero of legendary proportions, who has been kind to the God of Death, is finally here! When the Legend finally sees the God of Death, will he once again recognize that young, stubborn child of the past?

No! He won't recognize Cloud! It has been too long.

As that hero approached the teahouse, he walked by Wind and Cloud's table. Yet he did not show any sign of recognition, as if he had no inkling of who Cloud was. It was not because Cloud had changed so much, but rather… He does not know Cloud at all, and Cloud does not know him! He is not the one! He is not the black-clothed uncle Cloud had been waiting for.

The man who walked into the teahouse looked to be middle-aged. Much like the black-clothed uncle, his exact age was impossible to determine. This man had the same hair and style as the black-clothed uncle, but it was white. The robe was of the same cut as that of the black-clothed uncle, yet pure white.

Hence, the dust of the road laid heavy on his person, rendering his appearance even more worn and tattered.

This man was not all unlike the black-clothed uncle. Their features shared some semblance of their agelessness. And his voice, especially his sighs, were almost identical to the black-clothed uncle's. Even more similar was the look of weariness and sorrow, permeating from him. It is like the two of them shared the same fate, both capable of being a hero, yet neither wishing to be, until they fade…

Aside from the cloth and hair being of opposite color (black and white), this man could have sprung from the same mold as the black-clothed

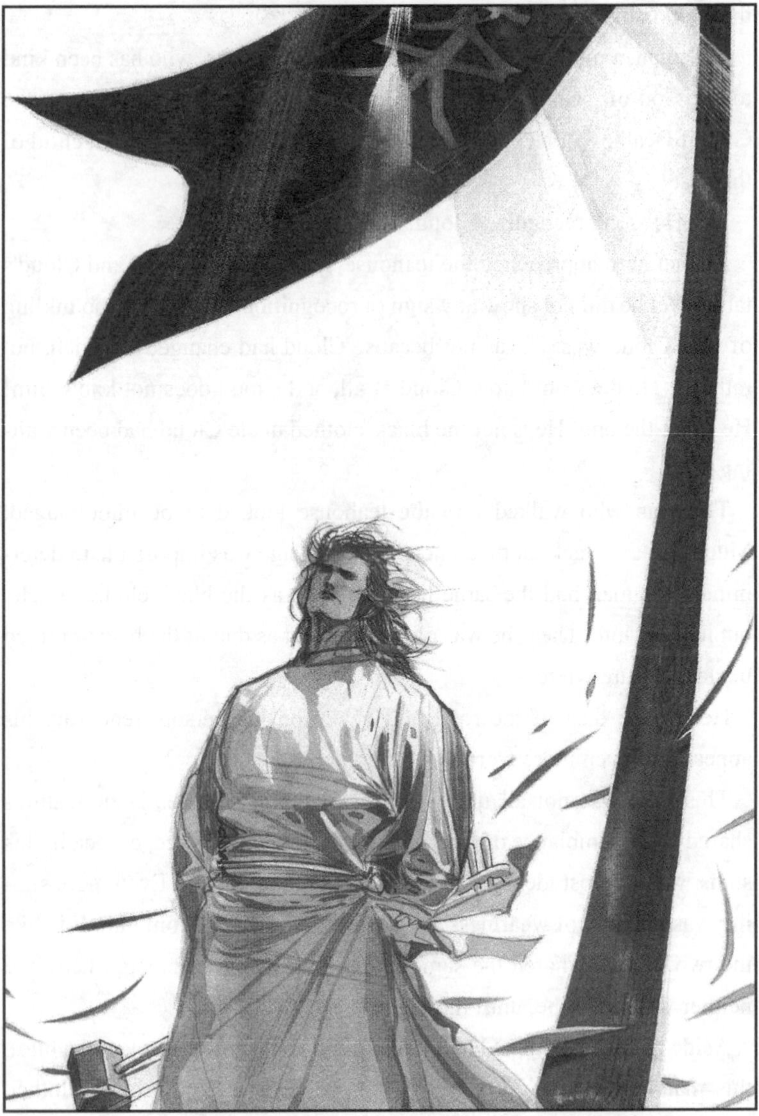

Uncle. From far away, they look to be the same person.

But even more shocking to Cloud was the man's mien of heroic proportions. It was not a feeling that normal people could sense, perhaps not even the Four Gentlemen of Long Mountain. Cloud's newly heightened senses allowed him to detect the same aura of invincibility and heroism as the black-clothed uncle. Moreover, Cloud was sure that this was the man who left the reserve of chi in the river to serve as a warning to those that hunted him, a warning to be left alone in his forsaken existence…

But how can this be? Cloud's heart went cold thinking that there was another like the black-clothed uncle, in mannerism, in mien, and in martial arts skill!

The only difference between them seemed to be one of feeling. The black-clothed uncle felt as if he were always retreating from the world, whereas this man felt as if he was at the ends of the world.

Yes, he is extremely shabby. His beard was dirty and matted; his white robe stained and tattered. In his hands was an old, worn down erhu. He had apparently come to this teahouse to sing of his lament as a way to earn a living.

The erhu in his hands looks to be very functional despite the long years of use. He has treated it as he would an old friend or companion…

True, who would travel on this long and lonely road with a bard! Through the rain, storms and misfortunes, is there something everlasting?

Perhaps, family, love…

Friendship.

The old erhu is like that old faithful companion, a treasured gift from maybe a beloved brother.

Though Cloud is disappointed that the man was not the black-clothed

Uncle, the Four Gentleman of Long Mountain still seem eager. They have never seen this legendary figure, who was rumored to have single-handily defeated the ten schools. They've only heard from stories that he had loose hair, a long robe and played the erhu. The man's extraordinary aura only added to the Four Gentlemen's belief that it was indeed him. Their swords were ready to fly out at a moment's notice.

Wind was also not disappointed. This was how he always imagined Uncle Ghost Tiger's master. He even played that same erhu song, and his legendary aura...

This man who came to sell his art seemed not to notice the eyes watching him. Walking straight to the counter, he lightly addressed the owner.

"Sir, hello."

His melancholy tone is just like the black-clothed Uncle. Although they were not the same person, their voice bespoke of a similar fate. Although they do not wish to be upon this world, there is something still tying them down--perhaps a brother that is extremely important. He still doesn't want to die or let go of that precious feeling...

The kind owner of the teahouse warmly welcomes the bard with a smile.

"Sir 'Erhu', you are late today. The travelers are lonely without your excellent tales!"

Erhu? That can not be his real name; who would be named after an instrument?

The white-robed bard answers: "I didn't feel well today, so I am a little late."

Wind looked to Cloud; this must be why the Four Gentlemen felt he was getting his just punishment. Was he really that hero that once domi-

46

nated the martial arts world? And now just a travelling bard, selling his songs for pennies?

The white robed man pulled up a chair after speaking with the owner. He prepared his erhu and was just about to begin a song, but…

Before he could utter a single note, a cold voice stopped him.

"Hold it! Is your name really Sir Erhu?"

It was the eldest of the Four Gentlemen of Long Mountain. He did not seem surprised with this interruption, as if he'd already glanced at all the people in the teahouse, including Wind and Cloud, and knew their purpose. He just did not feel the need to flaunt his knowledge.

He turned toward the speaker. "I am just a poor travelling bard; there is no need for real names. Of course, Erhu is not my real name, just a nick name used on the road."

"So then, what is your name?"

"Truthfully, I am a man down on my luck. I don't want to shame my parents by bringing up the name they've given me. Why do you press me so, good sir?"

The youngest, impatient with the older man's vague answers, laughed out loud.

"You are indeed down on your luck! But you deserve every bit of your misfortune! There's no need for you to pretend any longer! Do you know who we are?"

Erhu was quiet, as if too polite to speak out.

"We are the sons of Wan Chen, leader of the Long Mountain Clan. You killed my father when you attacked the ten schools. Today we will avenge his death with the 'Gentlemen Array' we created…"

The bard in white nonchalantly answered back: "Sorry, but I am really just a storyteller. I am not familiar with this ten schools. I am already down on my luck, please allow me to continue my livelihood."

The eldest of the Four Gentlemen spat out: "Hmph! Stop pretending! Though you are destitute, it does not make up for your past crimes! You think that you can get away with humiliating the ten schools so easily?"

"Today, no matter how you dispute the matter, you won't escape! Brothers… Gentlemen's Array!"

Under his command, the brothers drew the swords hidden in their sleeves and surrounded the white robed bard within a circle of steel!

The bard looked to the brothers and said: "Please sirs, whatever grievance you have, I sincerely apologize for them! I know that my death will not atone for anything, but please don't damage anything in this teahouse. They are good people here…"

But the four brothers were already set in their course of action, the eldest one commanding: "Damn it! We've vowed to spill your blood today, who cares about damaging some old furniture!"

"Attack!"

With his signal, the four brothers simultaneously moved.

In an instant, the white robed barb was surrounded in a net of swords, inescapable and oppressive.

What an impressive array! Though it is called "Gentlemen's Array," there is nothing gentlemanly about it. With the four brothers attacking at once, it is vicious and wicked, giving the trapped person no mercy, no quarter.

Wind and Cloud watched the array, and both thought of its power. No matter how skilled the martial artist, it would take them quite some time and skill to break out of this one.

Yet the white robed bard appeared nonplused. He continued looking around sadly, perhaps not realizing the true danger, or perhaps thinking it no threat.

He sat quietly and unmoved inside the array, as if awaiting death. The circle of swords begins to shrink. When it came within three meters of him, all four brothers struck out at once for the killing blow, a blow towards the bard's throat…

Is this the end of the battle?

Wind saw the swords pushing towards the bard's throat; the bard continued to sit unmoving. Is he hurt, or perhaps there is some reason why he can not attack? Just as he was planning to rush in and intervene with his speed faster than sound, Cloud put his hands on Wind's shoulder.

Wind quickly realized why. There was no need for his assistance.

In a flash, the bard's facial expression changed, from that of a reluctant man down on his luck, to a look of a master!

A legendary sword master!

That's right! Though different from Ghost Tiger's master, this man is perhaps another legend--a legend forced to reveal himself.

The four swords drew ever-closer, yet he sat still within the circle. Turning his head slightly, he lamented: "Ah… Gentlemen's swords, you are a set of four. You are called 'gentlemen,' so should you be used in a gentlemanly manner. Yet today you've fallen into the hands of four foul-mouthed, rude men. Swords! If you understand your fate, would you not feel sorrow?"

Swords and people not suited for one another?

After his speech, the bard looked with infinite sympathy towards the swords, and a strange thing happened!

A "BANG" rang through the swords, and the four Gentleman swords began to quiver, as if ashamed to face the bard. The swords continue to cower and shake, as if too embarrassed to continue…

The violent shaking left The Four Gentlemen ill-suited to retain a grip on their swords. With four loud "clangs," the swords flew from their hands and stabbed into the ground in front of the bard, swaying back and forth, as if bowing in shame in front of this legendary figure. The swords lost their luster!

And the four brothers, during their attack, felt the shaking of their swords. A strong surge of chi traveled up the swords through the grip and entered their bodies, disrupting the flow of their gathered chi. Suddenly they felt their knees go weak, and the four brothers fell kneeling towards the white-robed bard, unable to stand.

What a shocking turn of events! Wind surmised that this indeed must be the man who thwarted the ten schools. He couldn't believe that this man did not even have to raise a hand and already the enemies and their swords were bowing at his feet.

Cloud was even more shocked! He remembered when the black-clothed uncle use to bend the bamboo swords with just a glance. It was magically entrancing to him, that this man in front of him, with mere words, shamed the swords and had both the men and their weapons kneeling before him. He is just as powerful as the black-clothed uncle!

If his words truly caused the swords to bow in shame, then he was a legend, a legendary swordsman! Even the chi he used to cause the quivering in the swords was enough to make him a legend!

Eyeing the strange scene of the kneeling brothers, the customers in the teahouse were awed. The owner and workers especially; they never in

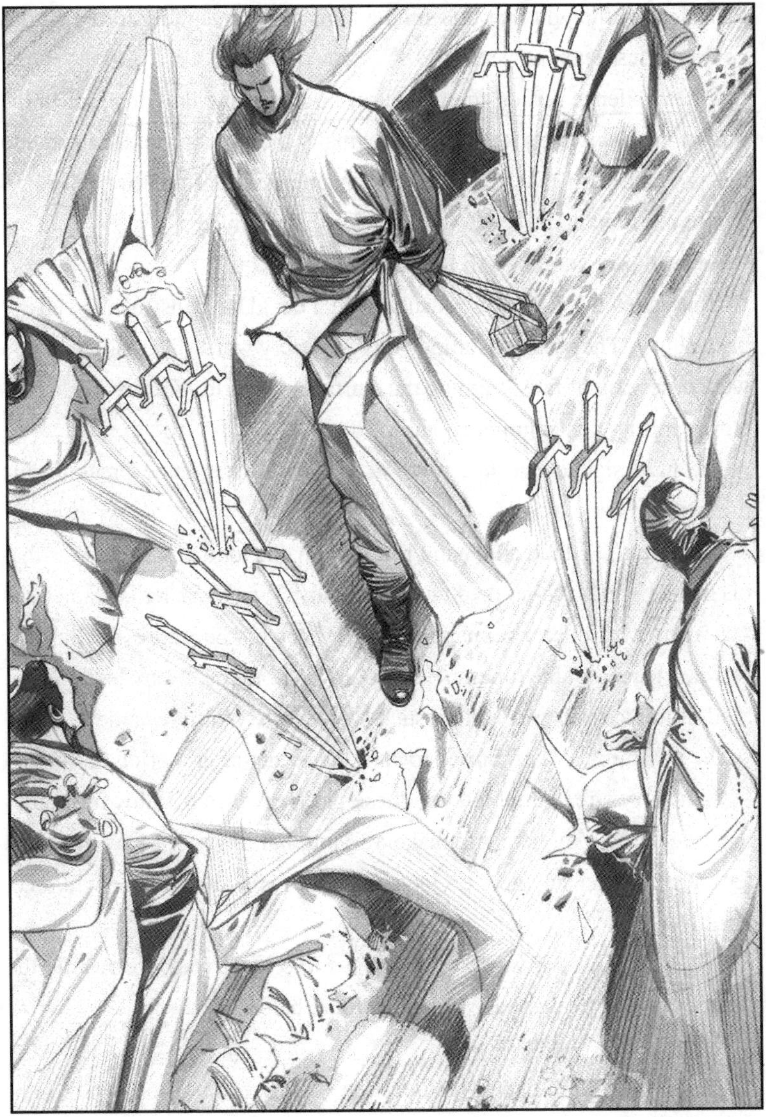

their dreams thought that this simple bard who came daily to tell stories could possess such power.

A dead silence fell on the teahouse; no one knew how to react to the turn of events. After a lengthy pause, finally the bard spoke. He looked to the sky and sighed deeply: "Ahh… Nameless, I promised you that I would not fight again, yet today, I broke that promise…"

He swallowed and bowed his head.

"But you know, if they just insulted me, I could have just swallowed my pride, but… They were insulting you with every word. They said that you were deserving of fate, shaming the martial arts world. You are my best… How can I let this continue… ahhh…"

The bard sighed one last time, as if he truly regretted breaking his promise to Nameless.

"Nameless"? Cloud and Wind heard the name loud and clear. Was that his name? The black-clothed uncle, or Ghost Tiger's master is Nameless?

A man who once commanded the respect of the entire martial arts world, a legend of the times... How could his name be "Nameless?" What kind of tragic story was behind such a deceptively simple name?

The white-robed bard turned toward the owner after a brief pause.

"I'm sorry sire, I troubled you these past few days by allowing someone like me to play here and make a living, but today… I have revealed too much... I can stay here no longer. I must leave. If fated we will meet again!"

And with that, the white-robed bard turned and walked towards the door, but when he passed Wind and Cloud, he paused…

He looked at Wind.

What is he doing? That is the question Wind asked himself! The white-robed bard looked to Wind with kindness and said: "Young man, thank you for wanting to help me out earlier. In this day and age, there are not many people willing to stand up against injustice… Heroes are fewer and fewer in number, ahhhh…."

Another long sigh! It seemed that sighing had already become a habit for this bard. Perhaps there was too much to regret in his past, causing him to turn a simple gesture into a habit.

Though he was pressed from all sides, he still had time to observe and see that Wind wanted to help. His power impressed even Wind and Cloud.

Then the bard's eyes fell on Cloud. Instantly, a light shone in the bard's eyes, as if he had discovered a treasure, or seen a shooting star. He turned towards Cloud gravely.

"That's strange, I can't see into your motives!"

It seems he's been paying attention to Cloud.

"This long-haired young man sitting next to you must be your Brother? I can tell that he has been practicing a long time. I feel he has the essence of broadsword about him, probably specializing in it."

He was right! Although Wind was known for his kicks, he had been practicing his family's broadsword style.

The white robed figure turned once again towards Cloud: "But you... You are surround by the chi of swords. And this sword chi, it seems very familiar to me, as if from someone I once knew. But you're so young, you couldn't have known *him*. Why do you have the same chi as him?"

With his questions, the bard suddenly reached out with his left hand.

"Young man, can I test something?"

Instantly, the bard's hands fell on Cloud's right shoulder. The speed of his reach was so fast, Cloud wouldn't have been able to dodge it, even if he tried. Cloud felt a surge of chi circling through his body, and suddenly it withdrew!

The white-robed bard looked with shock at Cloud.

"Impossible! How can you have some of his same chi? Are you related to him somehow? You are his son? Or perhaps his student?"

Cloud's body does have two types of sword chi. One is his family's style and the other is what he learned from the black-clothed Uncle, Endless Pain. Seeing the shock on the bard's face, Cloud knew that "he" must be the black-clothed Uncle. So breaking from his usual demeanor, he answered.

"I already know... who you are referring to. I wanted to... be his student, but it was not... fated to be."

The bard listened to Cloud's broken sentences; he seemed a little disappointed.

"That is a shame, it truly is."

"You are a sword of sorrow. You are a talent rarely found in a thousand years. If you can become his disciple, you would surely live up to his name. A shame, truly… Someone as talented as yourself, how could he bear to turn you aside?"

Cloud's usual cold demeanor showed a hint or regret.

"He didn't want me to be his student," Cloud responded, "because he was trying to help me."

"I understand."

"So I don't blame him. I only blame my own… stubbornness."

The bard looked to Cloud with warmth and admiration. Cloud spoke justly of a man who refused to take him on as a student.

"No! You are standing up for him even now. It was his loss that he did not take a student like you! Young man, don't be discouraged, with your talent, you can one day form your own style!"

The bard smiled.

"If 'he's' a legendary swordsman, then you will one day become a mythical swordsman!"

Wind couldn't understand what was going on, he always thought Cloud favored his Cloud Palms. He never knew that his brother once practiced the sword, or almost became "his" disciple.

Wind became more mystified of "him," and asked the bard: "Kind sir, excuse my rudeness, but Are you Ghost Tiger's master?"

Upon hearing the word "master," the white-robed man trembled. After another long sigh, he answered: "I'm sorry, young man. Although I share the fate of Ghost Tiger's Master, I am not lucky enough to be someone's master…"

Wind was stumped. "Then if you're not Uncle Ghost Tiger's master, then you are..."

Wind was planning to ask if the bard knew of Ghost Tiger's master, but before he could speak, the eldest of the four brothers spoke up with a sneer.

"Hahaha! I finally know who this bastard is!"

At this outburst, everyone in the teahouse turned towards him. The eldest brother's face contorted with a lurid look as if about to reveal some terrible news. There was no sign of any gentleman's manner.

With a smirk, he said: "I remember that my forefathers once told me the story of a man who was brother to the Legend. Someone just as powerful and similar in fate as that legendary swordsman, but who denied it all…

and betrayed the country for wealth! HAHAHA!"

A traitor? A serious crime! A crime not even a legend can wipe away. This white-robed bard who seemed so legendary in his own right, was a traitor? So…

He hides away from the world, pretending to be a travelling bard?

The bard heard the accusation, but he did not confirm nor deny it.

With a bitter smile, he said: "Betray the country? How much of the truth do you know? I do not need to justify my actions to you, nor do I need to defend my name…"

With that, he gave up the chance to explain and turned to leave. But the eldest of the four brothers would not let him go so easily.

"Hmph, birds of a feather flock together! The Legend's own brother betrayed his country, how much better could this Legend be? I bet the two of you planned it together." He then spat.

"Traitors!"

The words speared the bard like bolts of lightning. He turned back, stared hard at the eldest of the four brothers, and refuted: "No! He would never be a traitor!"

The bard did not care if the four brothers made light of his situation or good name, but when they marred his good brother's reputation, he immediately jumped to defend it.

"If you want to say that someone was a traitor, then it was me! 'He' merely let me go at the last moment! 'He' would never betray the country! I faced up to my sins; I will atone for them alone!"

The bard acknowledged all sins as his own. Why does he do so? Is it to protect someone else, Wind and Cloud pondered.

To deter his embarrassment, the eldest brother continued his relentless mocking.

"Heheh… are you saying that you are a traitor? You are just a worthless traitor!!"

The bard smiled bitterly once again.

"Yes, I was a traitor once, what of it? The people of the nation suffer under a cruel tyrant, he should have been betrayed long ago by a traitor like me!"

The eldest brother exclaims: "So finally! You admit it freely? Hehe… Fine, since we can't find that so called Legend, we can still avenge ourselves on his worthless brother!"

He turns to all the travelers in the teahouse.

"Sirs, you have all heard this man freely admit that he is a traitor! He should be condemned by all! If you love your country, then spit on this traitor!"

The owner and workers at the teahouse could never do such a thing, but the merchants began looking around in hesitation. It seemed that eldest brother's words had their intended effect of pitting the crowd against the bard.

In that moment of indecision, a cold voice rang out.

"I absolutely believe that he never betrayed the country!"

Those words were spoken by the normally taciturn and cold Cloud!

With this words, Wind stood up as well and spoke his mind.

"That's right! I believe that this man would never be a traitor!"

The eldest brother turned towards Wind and Cloud.

"So you say, but do you have any proof?"

Wind calmly explained: "This man has the air of a legendary sword master. Do you think someone who betrayed his own country could have such an aura? A good martial artist must learn to let go of worldly desires. If he has no worldly desires, what would he want of gold or jewels? It is inconceivable that he would betray the country for those!"

Yes! Wind is right! Although Cloud said nothing, he agreed with his brother's thoughts.

The eldest of the four brothers lashed out again. "You heard him admit to it himself! There's nothing you can say in his defense!"

Cloud and Wind glanced towards the bard to find a bitter expression on his face. Cloud felt to the depth of his own being that this bitter smile hid some incredible tale. A story so touching and tragic that none may understand what this man has gone through...

The white-robed bard seemed touched by Wind's kind words in his defense.

"I have told many tales here in this teahouse. But there has always been a story within my heart that I've never told anyone."

He paused, as if preparing to unleash some great burden.

"I was planning to take this story to the grave with me. Yet someone here is defaming my brother--that 'he' is a traitor! Although he has long passed away, he should not suffer such injustice. To clear his good name, it looks as if I must tell this tale..."

After his words, the bard looked wistfully at everyone through out the room, eyeing each person in passing. He began.

"This shall be the last story I will tell here. This story is about the entwining fate of two men, though they are not friends, nor enemies, nor brothers..."

With his words, the bard looked towards Wind and Cloud, as if he could sense that they were the same way, not quite enemies, friends nor brothers…

Next, he picked up that treasured old erhu, played the first notes of his sad song, and suddenly all seemed transported back to another time…

A string of names rushed to his lonely heart. A string of names tying to "him."

The first half of his life was like this string of names, turning round and round in his soul…

In his condition,

When all is down to nothing,

That string of names is…

Mu Long.

Xiao Yu (Little Happiness).

Monk King.

Sword Saint.

And a name that he will never forget in this lifetime:

Nameless!

Nameless was once known as:

"Ying Ming (Hero)," "Ying Ming…"

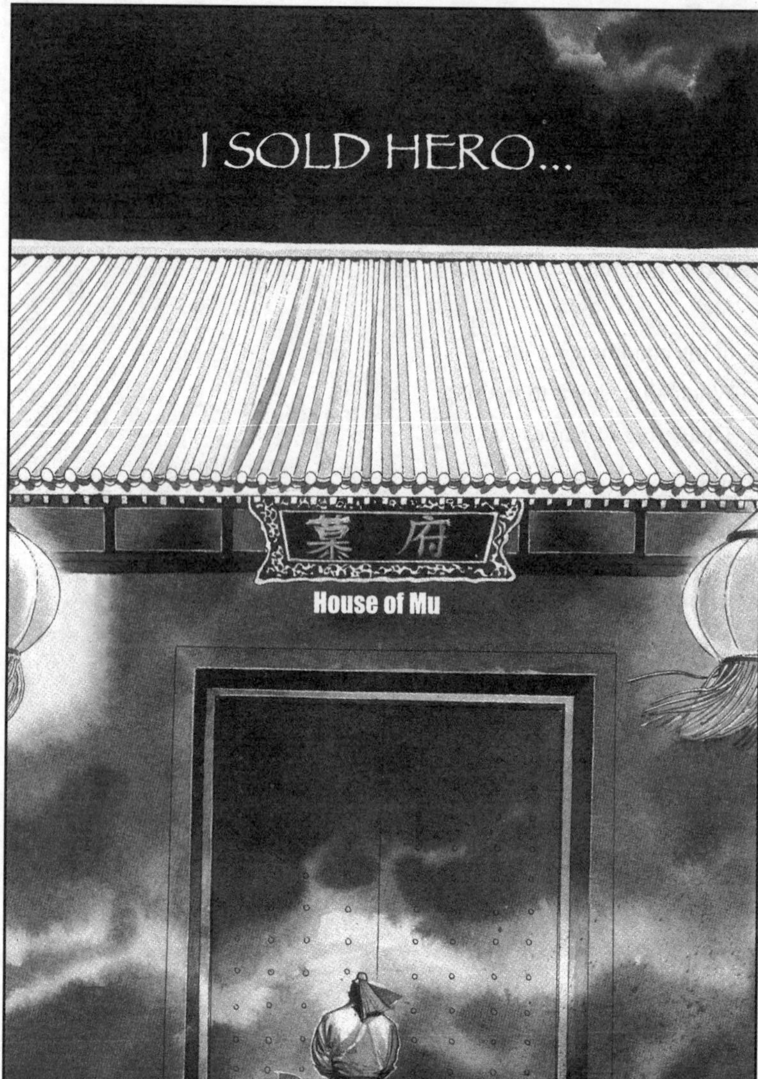
I SOLD HERO...
慕府
House of Mu

An unintentional sword,

Is often the true sword;

An unintentional heart,

Is often the true heart;

Perhaps, only an unintentional hero,

Can be a real...

Hero.

Many years ago, on a certain month,

on a certain day there was a nameless hero

admired by all.

His uncommon past, is a tale of yore.

The story of his life, revolved around a single enemy...

That enemy has a title feared and respected by all.

Sword Saint!

The Saint of Swords!

He never smiles.

He never smiles, because he has never been fully satisfied in his life.

Why has he never been satisfied? Because he had already achieved so much in a short amount of time.

He began learning the sword at age five. By age seven he excelled at the art. At age nine, his fame spread throughout the land. By age thirteen, he had obtained the highest level of swordsmanship and created his own style, the "Saint Sword". His powers grew with each passing day, none could come within three yards of him without his permission. From that time on, he remained undefeated!

Later, people respectfully termed him: Sword Saint! He had already transcended to the level of "Saint"!

Yet Sword Saint remained unhappy, because he was only twenty-seven years old. Twenty-seven and he had achieved ultimate perfection! What else was there to look forward too? What a terrible thought! So young to achieve such swordsmanship, respect and glory. He already had too much, what more could he hope to accomplish in this life? However… He still lives! Would he hold this title of "Sword Saint" to his grave? Is this the limit of his accomplishment?

No! He could not be satisfied with just that! He felt that, somewhere, in some corner of the world, there must be another swordsman as skilled as he. If he could battle that swordsman, it would bring his sword skill to the next level!

Is there such a swordsman in this world? Perhaps he doesn't exist? And Sword Saint, being the Saint of Swords, was he the pinnacle of the art form?

He does not know! And his uncertainty has led him to his current location.

The 27-year-old Sword Saint stood before a giant, ancient temple. He lifts his head to stare disrespectfully at the statue of Buddha within.

The ancient temple, named "Ni Ying Temple" is the largest in the surrounding regions. Sword Saint is not here to pray. He believes not in any God or deity. He deeply believes that fate is in one's own hands!

He came to the temple today to look for someone: the head of the temple. Monk King! The King of all Monks.

According to legend, the Monk King is a genius in Philosophy and

Medicine. He is the most respected monk in all the land, earning his title through his sheer skill and prowess.

Aside from his expertise in Philosophy and Medicine, he also has another talent. They say there is a small mirror embedded in his forehead. With it he can see through all mortal affairs on this earth.

Sword Saint comes to ask the Monk King to look for an opponent worthy of challenge. The "Unrivaled Sword" he holds is about to be sealed...

After a short time, a small monk emerges from one of the rooms on the east side.

"Lord Sword Saint, Monk King has refused all visitors lately. But upon hearing of your arrival, he said 'the one who comes is here,' and immediately instructed me to show you in. Lord Sword Saint, it seems that you are especially favored by the Monk King."

"Oh really?" Sword Saint refuses to engage in chitchat? Then why don't you stop your yammering and show me to the Monk King?"

The monk was merely trying to be friendly, but with Sword Saint's cold attitude, there was little he could do.

Then, a kind voice rang out: "It's time for your evening studies. Why don't you go and prepare. I will be host for Lord Sword Saint."

"The little monk couldn't wait to leave Sword Saint's presence. He hurriedly bowed and said: "Yes, master. I will go immediately to prepare."

This kind elder is Monk King? Sword Saint wrinkles his forehead in thought; from his kindly disposition and voice, one could already hear his infinite wisdom.

But Sword Saint has always been arrogant, and without a word of greeting, pushes open the doors to the chamber and walks in. At the end of the room sat a monk wearing plain cassocks. There was nothing special about the appearance of the monk, but his aura was kind and generous, much like the chi of a master martial artist.

"You, are you the Monk King who can see through all mortal affairs?" Sword Saint impatiently asks.

The Monk Kings pays no heed to Sword Saint's impudent tone.

"I am he," he replies calmly.

Sword Saint mocks: "Monks are suppose to forget all worldly desires, why do you hold the high and mighty title of King?"

The Monk King smiles and explains: "People are always looking for a leader. They look towards that person for answers and help. My name is merely a title to help those in need become interested in the study of Buddhism."

"You are good at making excuses. Since you are so wise, then you must know why I have made this journey to see you?"

"Lord Sword Saint, I can immediately tell you... There is... There is another who can challenge you."

Sword Saint, though ever-confident and arrogant was taken aback at the blunt and sudden reply. But part of his astonishment arrived from finally seeing the Monk King's face.

He was an elder man of about sixty years, with benevolent features. There was a small, thin mirror at the middle of his forehead. The light reflecting off the mirror seemed to pierce through everything, as if it really could see through all earthly and affairs. Sword Saint could see his visage in its center.

Sword Saint was surprised that the Monk King knew the exact purpose of his visit: to find a worthy opponent. Of course, the Sword Saint is no ordinary mortal, and quickly calms his surprised reaction.

"So you do know why I have come, Monk King! Then don't waste any more of my precious time! Tell me who is worthy of my challenge? Where is he now?"

The Monk King stared back at Sword Saint full of pity, as if seeing someone who is utterly lost. Sadly he says: "Sword Saint, why do you so desperately seek this person? Do you know that even if I were to tell you the whereabouts of this person, you would waste half your life waiting for him? Life is short, aside from the sword, can you not find another more meaningful way to live? Why must you waste your life away in such a manner?"

Sword Saint stares back defiantly. "HA! I live for the sword, and die by the sword! If I can't be the best, then why should I go on?"

Monk King tries again: "But even if you are the best, what does that mean?"

"Who knows, who cares!" Sword Saint yells, growing tired of the word games. Normally fear of him was enough to keep those around him quiet. He has never been questioned in this manner.

"It is the goal of all martial artist to become the greatest. If you cannot be the strongest, who would remember you? The loser only takes away shame, and in the end he will always be worse off than the victor."

"So tell me, who is this person? Where is he right now? Even if I have to search the whole world, I will battle with him!"

Monk King asks: "You won't regret this?"

"Ha! Even as the stars and moon turn, I will never regret this decision. I am not a person who EVER regrets!" Sword Saint replies without hesitation.

The Monk King replies: "But once you find that opponent, you will no longer be Sword Saint!"

"Oh?" Sword Saint begins to wonder, the impudence of this monk!

"An imperfect swordsman can no longer be called 'saint'. "Saint" implies never losing. It's not too late for you to turn back now."

"Monk King, this opponent you have found for me grows more interesting. Who is he?"

Monk King sadly sighs. Whether he is sighing for the soon-to-be-defeated of Sword Saint or for someone with a worse fate is unknown.

"He will become a legend. A hero surpassing all others, yet sadly his is a fate more cruel than all... A hero of the world, must experience all the troubles of the world..."

Sword Saint can't help but ask: "Someone more spectacular than me? Where is he now?"

With a hard stare at Sword Saint, the Monk King replies: "In a place far away, a place you can not yet find."

"Monk King! You are wasting my time with your senseless babble! Stop this nonsense and tell me clearly! Where is he?"

As if seeing a colossal mistake about to happen, the Monk King reluctantly replies: "I have tried my best to turn you away from darkness, yet you persist on this path of destruction. I suppose even saints face their own type of problems. Very well, I will tell you, the one you seek... is to the east! If you continue to travel east then you will find the opponent you seek. You don't need to know his name, when the time comes you will know! But you won't really find him, you will only find his past..."

His past?

The more he heard, the more confused Sword Saint became. It was enough for him to know that his opponent was to the east. He stood up impatiently.

"Okay, Monk King! I will believe you this time! But heed this warning…"

"You predicted that I would lose. I have taken this to heart and will avenge this shame. If I do lose, then I will admit defeat and live in seclusion. However, should I win, I will surely return…to level this temple and kill every living thing!"

With these words, the Unrivaled Sword in Swords Saints hand gleamed a pale light, lonely no more.

He has drawn his sword!

With a loud "WOOSH", the giant statue of the golden Buddha behind the monk was split in two by the power of Sword Saint's strike. Yet Monk King, standing between the Buddha and Sword Saint remained unharmed.

What terrifying swordsmanship! How did Sword Saint sunder the statue without harming the Monk King?

The Monk King remained supremely calm in the face of danger. Sword Saint "hmphed" once, then turned and walked away.

Looking at the fallen pieces of the Buddha, and again at the receding proud silhouette of Sword Saint, Monk King commented: "A pure Sword Saint heart, proud and relentless!"

"Do you know, no matter how good your swordsmanship becomes, your life will never be any better? You are going now to seek defeat. You will never escape your destiny, your fate… One time, one life, one day, if in one thought, you can give up your pursuit, and give up… Your sword!"

"But...Can you? Ahhh…"

Another long series of sighs follow. Finally the Monk King kneels

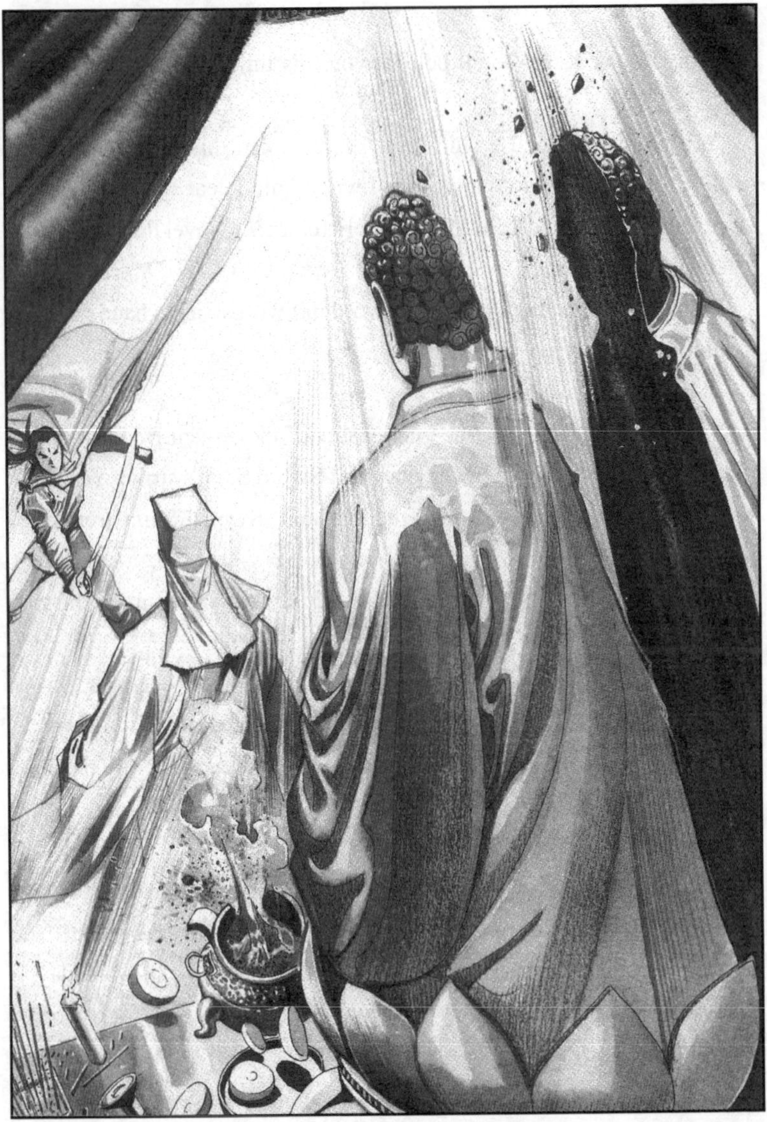

before the golden Buddha statue and begins his prayers.

He is not praying for Sword Saint, but rather for a child about to be born whose life will forever be linked with Sword Saint…

And another person.

Someone whose fate is almost identical.

They both face a cruel fate.

They both do not realize that their fate is not within their own hands…

Sword Saint continued to travel east. He passed village after town after homestead after community. The days went by, and without realizing it, he had already walked for half a month, yet still not a single clue came of this mystery opponent.

Although the trek was turning out to be fruitless, Sword Saint's proud nature prevented him from giving up. He continued to tell himself: "I will find him, my worthy opponent! That old Monk King knew why I was there, he said go to the east; it must be to the east! But why did he say I can only find his past?"

Half believing, Sword Saint continued travelling east, without any pause. His eagerness showing in every impatient stride.

As he thought, he continued walking and another half day passed. It was getting dark and Sword Saint began to look for a place to spend the night. Suddenly he saw up ahead, an intricately carved plaque, with the words "Mu Long Town."

"Mu Long Town?" he said. Sword Saint was well traveled and knew of this "Mu Long". Mu Long is actually one of the most famous generals in the emperor's army. This general had quite suddenly for some unknown reason, retired and took to his hometown.

Even so, the earnings he made as a general was enough for him to enjoy a lifetime of luxuries. The town ahead must be where he was living.

With the setting sun, Sword Saint doubted he would find lodging elsewhere, so with bold strides, he walked towards Mu Long Town.

Inside Mu Long Town, Sword Saint did not find any suitable inn. Instead, walking along the main street of town, he found that it ended in a giant structure.

Castle Mu!

A formidable castle! The front doors are made of solid bronze, at least the height of two men. The walls surrounding the castle were smooth and expansive, impeccably built. The grandeur and majesty of the structure suggested that it could only be the home of the retired general Mu Long. Though the Castle was grand by most standards, it meant nothing to Sword Saint! He came from the much more majestic Peerless City.

Sword Saint was just about to leave, when he found a strange phenomena in front of Castle Mu's doors. Hundreds of bamboo leaves lined up, forming an even half-circle around the doors, pointing inward, as if bowing to someone inside. A forest of bamboo surrounds Castle Mu. It's not surprising that the ground was covered with leaves, but the arrangement seemed too organized to be natural; it made Sword Saint pause in wonder. Suddenly the doors opened and two men appeared.

Not wanting to be discovered, Sword Saint leapt high into a tall pine.

The two servants with brooms swept aside the leaves as one servant grumbled to the other.

"Strange! These past months, the leaves have fallen like this everyday! It's like they're possessed. Of course we have to clean it up!"

"Shush! Fu! Be careful! If the Lord heard you, you're gonna get a beat-

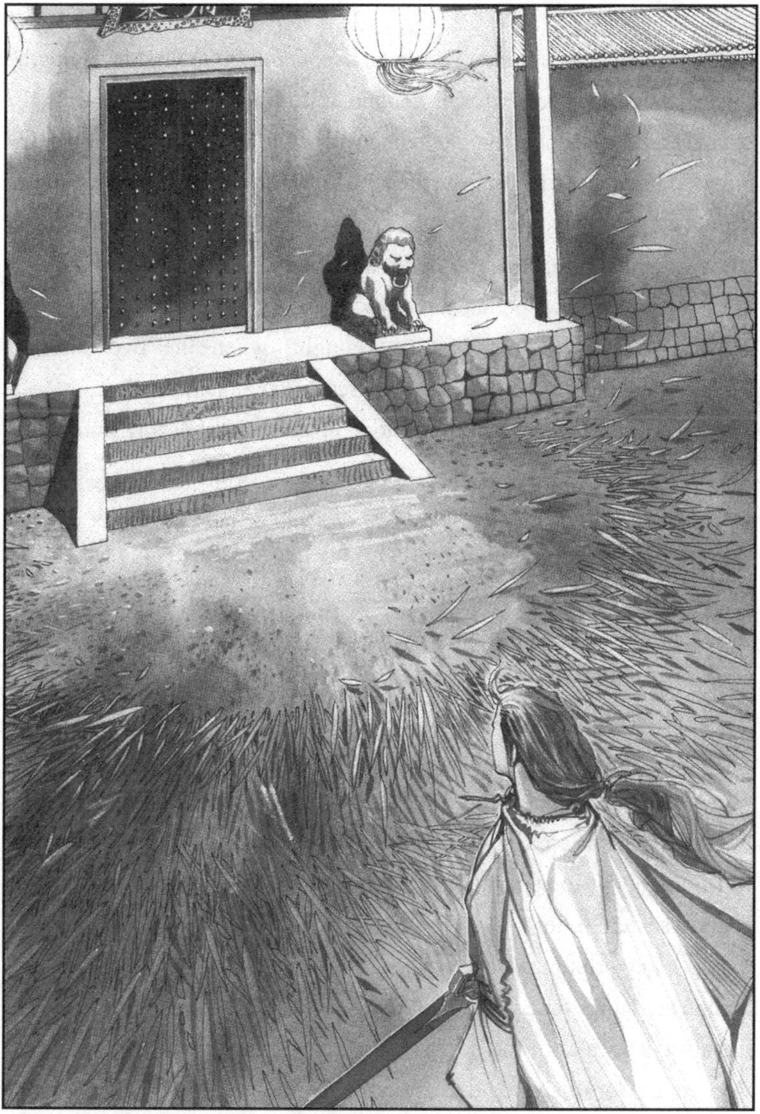

ing!"

So this strange phenomena has been happening for the last half-month? Sword Saint seemed to recall a popular folk superstition regarding a strange natural phenomena that coincided with the birth of extraordinary individuals. Legend had it that when the famous general Yue Fe was born, a giant condor flew overhead at the exact moment. The origin of his name came from that bird. Now the leaves are lined up in front of the Castle, in the shape of a sword, perhaps?

Sword Saint was absorbed in thought, when the two servants exclaimed: "Oh, it's the Lord and Mistress! Welcome home!"

With that, the two servants both stood up and bowed deeply from either side of the doorway.

How imposing, even though General Mu Long has retired, he still expects his servants to treat him with utter respect. This piqued Sword Saint's curiosity and he stayed to learn more.

At that moment, Sword Saint suddenly felt an energy assailing him. A strong force that pushed at him!

It's the feeling of a sword! The ruler of all swords!

Sword Saint has met numerous swordsmen in his battles, yet none have ever given him such a feeling! It felt like an announcement, that the ruler of all swords was arriving and about to walk through the doors. Is General Mu Long about to appear? Is he the opponent Sword Saint had been so eagerly searching for?

The hand gripping the Unrivaled Sword began to sweat. This is a unique sensation for Sword Saint. He has been in countless duels and he has always been calm and decisive. Yet here is someone possibly stronger than he, a ruler of swords that gives him pause.

A giant, muscular man walked out of the doors. He seemed about forty years of age with a square face and strong jaw, eyes like an eagle and broad, thick eyebrows. This was the face of power and authority. It must be General Mu Long.

Although General Mu Long looks strong, there was no way he could be that ruler of swords. There was no sword chi coming from him at all, only the chi of a palm strike specialist. This general is an expert in palm forms. That air of swordsmanship does not come from him!

Then where is it coming from?

Sword Saint pondered with a sense of suspense, his eye fell on the person walking behind General Mu Long. Madame Mu!

There! With Sword Saint's prowess, he instantly deduced that powerful swordsmanship aura was emanating from none other than... Madame Mu!

Madame Mu was a beautiful, kind woman in her thirties. She looked to be delicate and fragile, not the type associated with a master swordsman. Then Sword Saint begins to sense that the powerful chi is actually coming from her stomach!

She is six months pregnant!

That is when Sword Saint realized, the natural phenomena, and the powerful chi all point to the birth of this child. Even before birth, the child is strong enough to attract Sword Saint; how will he be when he is born? No wonder the Monk King warned Sword Saint that he could only find his opponent's "past". A child, before he becomes a legend... That is his past...

Just as the Monk King predicted, it would take the Sword Saint long years of waiting before he could fight this opponent... Still, Sword Saint was not willing to give up this chance. He had searched for so long, he could not just let it go. It was hard to find anyone in the wide world to share something with, be it a lover, a friend, or an enemy... So even if he had to wait nineteen years, over 7000 somewhat meaningless days, Sword Saint would wait, to prove that the Saint is still the best!

Madame Mu beamed with pleasure as she walked through the doors.

"It's been so long since I've been this happy. I'm cooped up all day inside where it is dark and depressing. Longing for when we will be able to live a truly carefree life."

The bearded General Mu Long did not immediately respond. He felt guilty. These years, he had battled far and wide, earning him the wrath of many enemies. Now that he had finally retired, he now had to worry about enemies seeking vengeance. His fierce palm strikes would deter many, but what about his wife? She does not know any martial arts, so for her protection she had to stay inside as much as possible. Madame Mu lived as a caged bird.

Aware of her husband's sudden silence, Madame Mu knew what troubled him. So she steered the conversation towards another topic.

"That's right! You know Autumn's house around the back? She is also six months pregnant, and I think we might give birth around the same time. I wonder how she's doing?"

"Ah, wife! They're just peasants! You don't need to worry for them. They are so lowly, and should not be compared to our child! You best forget about her, before you upset your pregnancy."

Madame Mu kindly interjected: "It's not like that. Autumn, she's so poor. She is a hard-working woman, but her husband is a louse. He gambles and drinks away her hard-earned money. She's six months with child, yet still has had to sew day and night to make ends meet. Last time I went to visit them, I felt so sorry for her. I tried to give her some money, but she's too proud, refusing to take handouts. She also said that her child will be as brave as her. Even as a woman she still had her pride and integrity. I wish I could go see her again…" Her eyes filled with a sad look.

"My dear! Why do you waste your time worrying for these lowly peasants? There are sorry women like her all over the world. I just don't know why her miserable hovel has to be leaned right up against our back wall! I wish that I could throw them out!"

It appears that General Mu Long believes in his supremacy and looks down on those not in the same class as he, but Madame Mu thinks otherwise.

"No! Long! You can't do that to her! She's already barely scraping by, if you do this, how can I bear it?"

General Mu Long feared upsetting his wife during her pregnancy, so he quickly lied.

"Worry yourself no longer with this, my dear. Why don't you go back and rest some more. It's dangerous for us to stay out here for too long…"

He barely finished the sentence, when a dangerous feeling approached! Mu Long heard a loud sound behind him and the gleam of a sword approached!

General Mu Long has encountered thousands of battles; he is a strong man. He moved two fingers to parry the oncoming blade, but when he looked down it wasn't a sword. It is a thin piece of paper!

To make a thin paper feel like a sword blade is incredible! The attacker must be a great swordsman! Mu Long scanned the surroundings, yet there was no one there. The attacker must have scurried away quickly.

The general opened the letter to find a few lines of heart stopping words written within.

Natural phenomena outside your castle,
a hundred bamboo leaves bowing toward a king of swords;
19 years hence,
Sword Saint will battle with your son!

Penned by Challenger -- Sword Saint

Sword Saint! Mu Long's heart sank! The world famous Sword Saint believes that his son will be a master swordsman? In nineteen years, he will come to fight a duel?

Although powerful, General Mu Long has heard enough of Sword Saint to know his reputation is real. He felt a twinge of fear, and his wife saw it in him.

"Long, what's happened? You don't look good, what did that note say?"

"Don't worry about it, my dear! It's just some children playing a prank! It's getting late, let's head back inside."

He hurriedly led Madame Mu inside.

Egotistical Sword Saint is. He felt that he had enough power to defeat anyone.

But it's just that this time, his challenger's letter was left in too much of a hurry. Because the one that he would eventually tangle with, might not be the child within Madame Mu's womb!

The child within Madame Mu may very well be a real ruler of swords, yet in the world there is something higher than a ruler that is…

A heavenly sword!

A heavenly sword. Mighty as a sword ruler! Perhaps the "Sword Ruler" and the "Heaven Sword" will become friends...

This Heavenly Sword has also not yet been born, hidden inside the womb of another woman. That woman lives behind the castle...

Night grows deeper, colder. Autumn's eyes are starting to blur.

She pushes aside her drowsiness, sewing her hopes and dreams into the clothes she's making. She just needs to save a little more for her unborn child.

Her home is situated behind the grand Castle Mu, yet it is shabby beyond belief. She never blames fate for her situation, after all, she picked a gambling, alcoholic for a husband: Wei Yaozhu. A poor home becomes even worse...

"Yaozhu" means "glory to the family," it s a common name encompassing the hope of parents. Yet Yaozhu has no such intention in mind. If he even tried a little bit, this home would be better. Still, Autumn didn't blame him. Like tonight, he was lounging with his legs propped up on the table, drinking his wine. She made no complaint. Actually she was too busy with work; she has to complete these clothes before tomorrow morning.

Seeing her squinting and struggling with her work, Yaozhu impatiently began yelling,.

"Hey! Why are you still up? You know I have to sleep even if you don't!"

Autumn tried to answer.

"Yaozhu, don't be so hard on me! I'm just trying to do a little bit extra for our unborn child. It's our first child, I just want to be prepared."

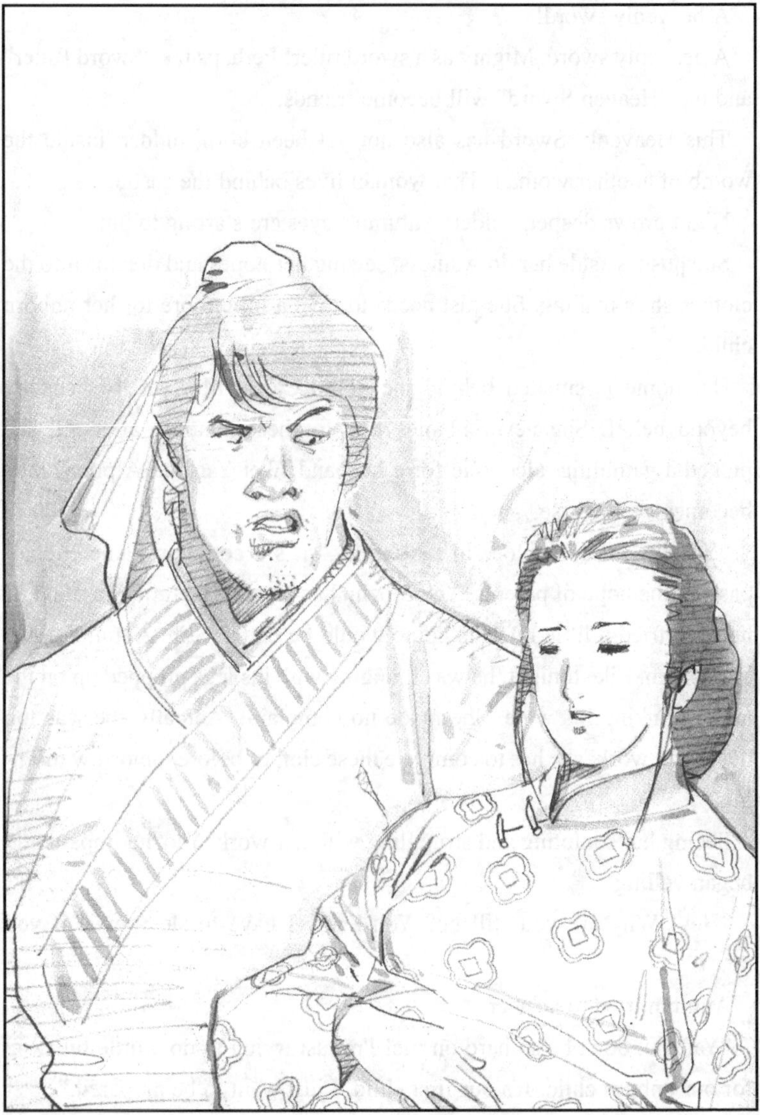

"Really?" Yaozhu responded. "Well, you're the one who wanted a baby anyway. I never agreed to it. I told you to take some herbs and get rid of it! See, look around you! We don't have a thing. We're already poor enough and can't feed another mouth..."

Autumn gently rubbed her burgeoning stomach and said: "No! I have this strange feeling. I know that our child will be a boy, and when he grows up, he will be a great hero!"

"Yaozhu, I've already thought about it. If it's a boy, can we name him Hero"?

"Hero?" Yaozhu laughed. A father such as he could not conceive of having a heroic son.

"Ha! Forget about it! We're lowly commoners; we would never give birth to someone like that! You're dreaming!"

But Autumn insisted.

"No! Even the worst person in the world can achieve more if he tries. Yaozhu, you're about to become a father, think kindly if not for yourself, then maybe for our child..."

Hearing her unintended criticism, Yaozhu was angered.

"Forget it! I'm going to try my luck at a few games. Since you're so great, you'll figure out what to do for our future!"

With that he was gone, slamming the door behind him.

"Yaozhu!" Autumn shouted after him. But it was already too late. Her words fell on deaf ears. She wanted to have a serious discussion about the child, yet he continues to ridicules her. Now the shabby house felt even lonelier as she sat alone amongst a pile of unsewn clothes…

She has already suffered so much for the child. At six months, just when she needed his support the most, her husband abandons her. She must toil alone, mending clothes all through the night...

How can men be so cold-hearted?

Though she had to work even harder, she didn't feel lonely. Her child was keeping her company...

She smiled, and caressed her stomach.

"Child, you are so poor. Even before you are born, your father already doesn't want you. But don't worry about that. I will take good care of you... No matter how poor we get, or how much I have to work, I will give birth to you and raise you. I believe that life is your own. Your fate has not been determined; you can still be something great. You won't be like your parents, you...will be a HERO!"

Her strong belief intact, Autumn picked up her sewing and began again. Every thread paving the road for her unborn child...

Will this child's life be as his mother wishes?

Will he become that legendary hero?

One night, as Autumn lay awake, in a vastly better surrounding, another woman tossed and turned--the wife of General Mu Long.

Mu Long had been worrying incessantly over Sword Saint's letter. He called in his advisor Bao to discuss what could be done.

"Bao, this Sword Saint, his reputation precedes him. He will come nineteen years hence. How can we best handle this situation?"

Bao, the strategist had been a longtime follower of General Mu, and a shrewd person with keen insight. He immediately thought of an idea.

"Master Mu, it is quite simple, really. If the child within your wife's womb is really destined to be a ruler of swords, what will you do?"

Mu Long thought for a while before responding. "Of course I would treasure him and never allow him to accept the challenge, even if he were the ruler of swords. I don't know how he might fare against Sword Saint, and I still need him!"

Bao smiled and said: "There's no need to fear! Sword Saint has not seen the child. If you found someone to substitute as your son, Sword Saint won't know."

Mu Long started to understand.

"So you mean…"

With a whole-heated laugh, Bao continued.

"Well, Sir, if you had, say, another son, a son that you cared nothing about... maybe another boy the same age, whom you taught martial arts to..."

Mu Long laughed: "Haha! I see it now, I will have an adopted son. Then when Sword Saint comes to fight, my true son has nothing to fear, he will never be in danger."

"Exactly!"

"But where will I find a son? Who would let their child go in my son's place?"

"Haha… Master Mu, there is nothing you can't buy with money in this world. There will be some parents willing to sell their child. It is but a simple matter."

"A substitute? Hahaha…"

Bao's plan seemed sound and Mu Long was finally relieved.

But was he rejoicing a little too soon?

Never in his wildest dreams could he have imagined that this adopted son would turn out to be much more than he bargained for. A son he would try to put aside and not care for. And not until he lay dying, would he discover just how much he really cared for this adopted son…

Time flies by in the blink of an eye...

Madame Mu finally gives birth to a boy. That night the winds howled, and all the leaves from the nearby forest were blown toward the Castle as if in homage to the birth of a great persona...

As Sword Saint predicted, could he really be the ruler of swords? Mu Long didn't know! He just knew that his son had a look of power about him--for certain he would grow to be a strong man!

Mu Long named his son Hiro, a hero that will be.

The boy named Hiro enjoyed all the luxuries the world had to offer. Mu Long had a special robe tailored for him and even made matching silver shoes.

In a dark corner, relatively going unnoticed, there was another child born at the exact same moment. Their conditions were a world apart.

That night, Autumn was up late working again. She tried to finish the clothes in the dying lamplight. She did not have any more money for oil, so when the light went out, she would not be able to finish until tomorrow.

These couple of months, Autumn's stomach had grown larger. It became increasingly difficult for her to move around. Her hands were not as quick and her eyes not as sharp, so an already shabby home becomes even more barren.

Yaozhu still did not bring any money home. He continued gambling away what little money he received. Autumn continued her struggles alone because...

Just then came a wrenching pain!

"AH!" she moaned. It was time! Her child was about to be born!

But there was no one to help her, she was utterly alone...

In the wide world, there was only her and her child…

She struggled, and the meager lamp was knocked from the table, and went out. She didn't have time to lie on the bed, the pain weakening her so. She remained as she fell on the ground, in the dark, her child emerging into a world of darkness…

A baby's cry echoed through the hovel. Finally, she had finally given birth to him! The child had a thin body. In the darkness, Autumn felt like it was something much larger. Something maybe not even human…

Why did she feel that way?

Autumn pushed up her weakened body and relit the lamp. With the light, she looked down at the child in her arms.

"AHHH!"

It' was not a child she's holding. It was not even human!

It's…

A foot long Sword!

A mighty sword!

Her shock was great! How could I give birth to a sword, she thought?

She tightly closed her eyes in fright, and when she opened them again, a strange thing happened! That sword she saw was gone. In her arms was a baby, a baby boy!

After crying once, the baby was silent. As if he knew that he was meant for something more in this world.

Although the boy did not cry, he did not appear to be cold or unfeeling. His eyes shone like stars, and his face spoke of great power. With his small hands, he reached up to caress Autumn's cheeks, and Autumn felt her heart calm.

Perhaps she was just weakened from the birth and her eyes were playing tricks on her... *how can one give birth to a sword?*

She calmed a great deal after that, and kissed the baby lightly.

"My son, you are finally here! Do you know how much I've waited for this day? Although your father ridiculed me, I knew that you wouldn't disappoint me..."

The baby seemed to understand her words. His small eyes looked up into hers with a flicker of sorrow, as if he felt sadness for all she had gone through...

Suddenly, the door was kicked open!

It's Yaozhu!

"Yaozhu?" Her husband stank of alcohol, and Autumn knew he must have been out drinking again; but today she gave birth, so she tried to be cheerful.

"Yaozhu! You're back! Look, it's our son! It's a boy! Let's call him 'Hero'!"

Yaozhu's face was pale, and his hair lay in a dripping mess. Autumn noticed that it was pouring rain outside.

"Ah! It's raining outside? Yaozhu, come in! Don't catch a cold."

She was still weak from her birth, yet she didn't worry for her self, she worried first for her husband. No matter how he treated her, she still loved him! Though they are poor, her only hope was that the three of them could be a family together... She could never imagine that this happy night would soon turn into a nightmare!

Yaozhu said nothing, merely standing outside. With a stiff expression he asked: "Is that... Hero?"

Hearing her husband call the baby Hero, Autumn was ecstatic! She smiled.

"Yes. Yaozhu... so you like this name too?"

Yaozhu didn't answer the question.

"Let me hold him."

Autumn was taken aback, she thought Yaozhu was acting very strange. But of course any father would want to hold his newborn son, so she gave Hero over to him.

Yaozhu didn't look at the baby in his arms, as if they had no relation with one another. He suddenly turned and began walking back out into the rain!

Autumn was shocked, she ran after them.

"Yaozhu! What…are you doing? Where are you taking Hero?"

Yaozhu turned with a cruel smile.

"Stop yammering! Let me tell you… I've sold Hero!"

What? He… sold Hero?

Autumn stood thunderstruck! The rain relentlessly pelted her fragile body. The baby in Yaozhu's arms was soaked through, yet the boy did not cry out even once. As if he did not want to bend to fate!

Desperately, Autumn sprang forward with all her might, holding on to Yaozhu, she cried: "No! Yaozhu! How can you sell Hero? How can you sell your own son? Give Hero back to me!"

"No way! Hero is my son! I'm his father! I have the right to sell him if I want to! I can sell him to whomever I please! I already sold him for three taels of silver! You can't stop me!"

Three taels? This child filled with Autumn's hopes, sold for three taels? So little for so much.

How shameless. Not until now does he admit that Hero is his son. But who was it who suffered through ten months of pregnancy? Who sewed

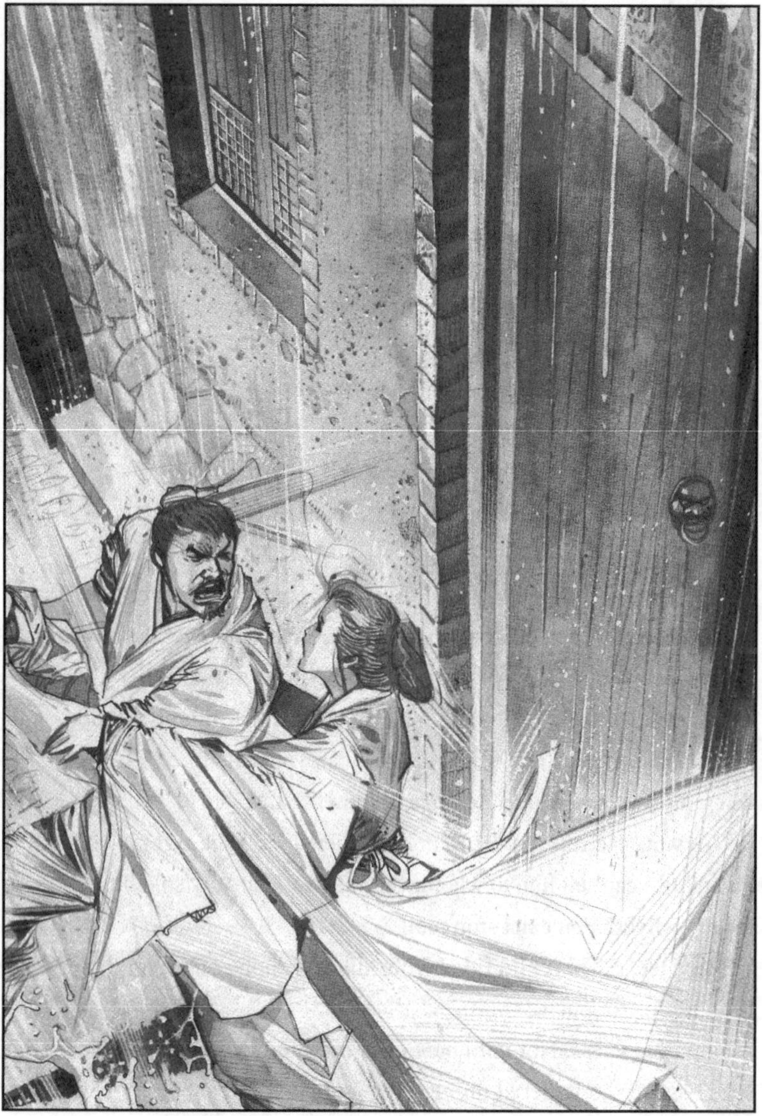

through day and night to make a living? Who believed in their son? Who said he would grow up to be a great hero?

Now this feckless man comes back, claiming to be the "father." Without an ounce of regret, he sells the child… for 3 taels.

No! Autumn doesn't want to lose her baby! If her son were sold, then his life is over! She can't let that happen!

Gathering the last of her strength, she grabs on to Yaozhu, not letting him move even half a step! She won't allow him to sell her precious baby! Her Hero!

Yaozhu didn't count on facing Autumn after her difficult labor and grew angry. With reckless abandon, he throws her aside and stomps on her stomach as she lay on the ground. Instantly blood spewed from her mouth as her head was smashed against a boulder. Yet she still clang on, crying: "No! Yaozhu! Don't sell my baby! I beg you, don't sell Hero! Yaozhu, you're destroying your own son! We haven't even done anything for Hero… Don't… do this. Our son… we have to… raise him…"

Yaozhu, seeing her clinging on, started to feel a little guilty. While she was still struggling to stand, he ran without turning around, despite her cries ringing in his ears.

He ran in the rain and looked down at the baby in his arms. He suddenly spit in the child's face!

"Ha! Little bastard! Your mother has high hopes for you! But will you really be a hero? I am your father, so I think you can just forget about that! I've sold you already; we'll see if you'll ever be a hero? Or maybe you will spend the rest of your life as a slave or servant? HAHA, at least you'll make your father a little drinking money!"

His cold-blooded laughter was soon covered by the thunder as if the heavens were angered by his worthlessness!

Who did he sell his son to? Where?

The child in his arms, whose name should be Hero, looked up at his father. It was not a look filled with hatred, nor did it have any child like innocence…

The boy's eyes were filled with sorrow and regret.

Regret and sorrow for a father who would lose everything for the sake of money! A father who would willingly give up his only son!

Blood and tears, mingled together by the rain. Autumn had finally risen to her feet. Yet she did not chase after Yaozhu, she merely stood up and began walking. One step, then another, without any clear direction...

Everything else was of little importance! Her son, her son had been taken from her. What else is there for her in this world?

Yet she still stood up. Her eyes look…

Is she? Has she gone mad?

The shock of losing her son and the blow to her head was too much for her. Her eyes filled with tears, her body covered in blood, wet and bruised, her head ringing... She could bear it no longer! Her mind was lost to her!

However, she continued to walk forward, talking quietly to herself.

"My…son, where are you? No matter who you've been sold to... No matter where you are, don't forget that I love you! My heart will always be with you... Don't forget my hopes for you…You have to… become… A…Hero! Don't be like your father! Don't let him look down on you! Don't forget the pain that I suffered…You have to grow up to be a good person, a wonderful man. You have to become a hero…A legendary… hero!"

She repeated this to herself over and over again as she walked through the rain. The confidence and hopes of a loving mother!

Autumn disappeared that night. She disappeared from Mu Long Town, and none knew where she had gone.

The cold rain only seemed to emphasize the tragic affair of the evening. A child abandoned by his father, without a mother... A child sold...

Who will care for him now?

Who?

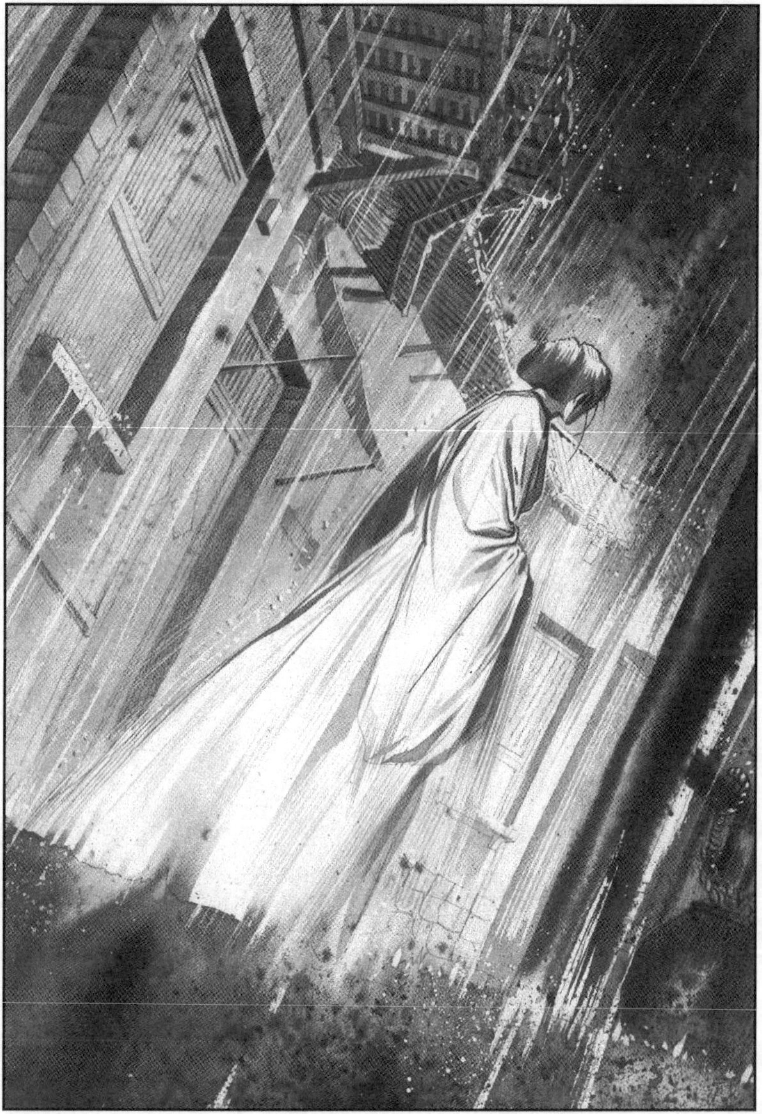

Regardless,
"Undefeated" is his - sword!
"Losing" is his - fate!
Victory comes with the sword.
Hatred comes with the sword!
Hero, Ying Ming, Nameless...

Swords Sunder The Lands
Heroes Through The Times

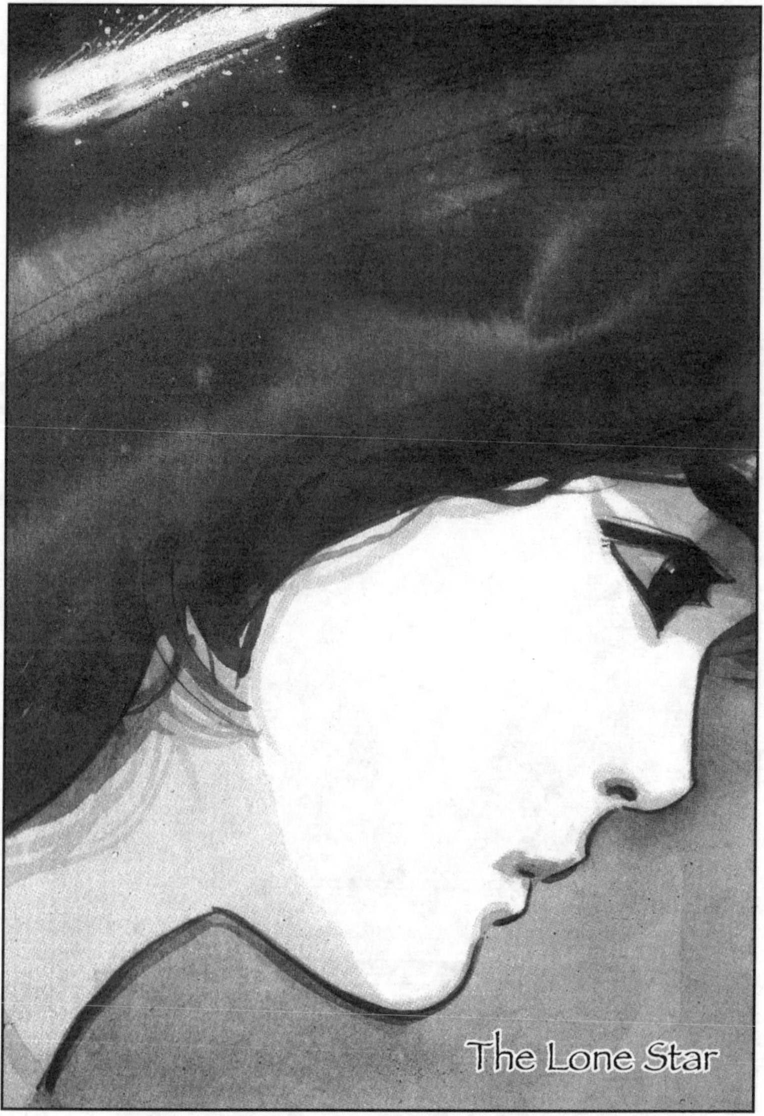
The Lone Star

In time,

In this world,

In this life;

"Her" life has always been intertwined with two men.

These two men unwittingly pull her life's "happiness and sadness."

And her, between the three of them, there is no hatred, only admiration and understanding.

"She" was only ten when she met them.

An unforgettable ten.

"She" even met them in an unusual way.

She met them in a painting.

An old faded painting.

She will never forget when her father pulled out that old painting from underneath the bed. The first glance was enough to entrance her.

The piece was painted by her father ten years ago.

In this world, nothing escapes the ravages of time.

The painting has grown old and faded.

Every person and object in the painting has faded, with the exception of two people. Their lines and colors remain sharp and clear, the luster shining still, even with the passage of time.

It is their painting that has so transfixed "her!"

The two people are two small children.

Two-month old babies.

"Xiao Yu!"

A string of children's voices called out at the same name, and the girl Xiao Yu is currently sitting on the steps in front of her house, looking intently at the old painting.

Xiao Yu is ten-years old.

Despite her age, her beauty shows through. With large almond eyes, a perfectly shaped mouth, and her cheeks glowing with a pretty pale pink, she had the makings of a "true beauty."

But the young beauty did not appear energetic, at least not when compared to the happy, boisterous children playing outside her home. She seemed content sitting in a corner alone, enjoying the painting.

The sun was about to set, and the children had been at play for much of the day, just as Xiao Yu had been staring at the painting for most of the day. Finally a girl in bright reds and greens steps up to her.

"Hey! Xiao Yu! It's almost dark! Why do you keep looking at that old picture? Father painted it ten years ago. He just took it out to show us today, but you don't need to be so into it!"

The girl speaking was an eleven year old named Chiu Hong. She was actually Xiao Yu's older and only sister.

The other children also chimed in: "Yeah! Xiao Yu! You're always so quiet! You're even quieter today! What's so great about that dumb old picture?"

The young Xiao Yu smiled, showing a kindness rarely seen in children her age. She shook her head gently.

"No. This pictures is… not ordinary at all."

Chiu Hong laughed. "Sis! I know that you're into the arts, especially the erhu and painting, but this painting isn't even father's best work. Why are you so into it? I looked at it, and it's not that great."

Xiao Yu continued to look at the picture, and answered: "Sister, do you know when father painted this picture?"

Impatiently, Chiu Hong replied: "I know that! My father painted this when he attended the one-month birthday celebration of our cousin. Father painted the scene he witnessed that night. You were not yet born then, and I was only one-year old. Later that year, mother gave birth to you and passed away."

Yes! The painting in Xiao Yu hands shows a festive banquet. Guests fill the seats and the halls are filled with cheerful décor. A middle-aged couple holding a baby boy is the focal point of everyone's attention.

Xiao Yu recalled: "Yes, that's it. Father told me that when he returned home he tried to paint as quickly as possible the scene he saw. There was someone who inspired him there..."

"Who?" Chiu Hong asked. "Uncle Mu Long is our mother's older brother. Although our family is not that poor, it's nothing compared to Uncle Mu Long's castle! I heard that Uncle was a famous General in court before his retirement. His castle must have been pretty impressive, to inspire Father to paint this!" Her eyes filled with longing. It appeared that Chiu Hong was not satisfied with her own house.

"That's not it." Xiao Yu replied.

"Father said, he drew this painting because he met our uncle's two sons..."

"Two sons?" Chiu Hong asked. "Doesn't uncle only have one son?"

Xiao Yu answered: "That's how it was. When Uncle's son was born they found another baby boy abandoned outside their door. The abandoned baby had a small jade pendant with the word 'Hero' carved on it. The boy's parents must have wanted to name him Hero. They were probably so poor they couldn't afford to keep him. Father heard Uncle say that when they found the boy, his umbilical cord hadn't even been cut. He was probably a newborn baby. Since they were born on the same night, Uncle decided to adopt the abandoned baby boy…"

Chiu Hong cut in with: "See, our Uncle is a generous man! That bastard boy is so lucky, to be the adopted son of such a great man." Jealousy filled her tone. Though her father was still alive and well, she wished to be adopted by her rich uncle as well.

The "bastard" named by Chiu Hong was the abandoned baby in the painting, Xiao Yu hurriedly defended him.

"Sister, how can you say that? His parents abandoned him; its really sad!"

Chiu Hong pouted. "Sis, you're always so soft-hearted. I won't argue with you anymore! Speaking of which, it's just a painting of a banquet, what so great about it?"

Xiao Yu pointed at the picture, and answered: "Because of him!"

Him? Who?

Chiu Hong and the gathered children looked closely at the painting. At first glance, they saw amidst the guest-filled banquet what seemed like a star!

The star light came from the baby boy held by her Uncle!

Although just a month old, the baby boy already showed his magnetic personality, as if he was born to be a great person.

Chiu Hong quipped: "Ha! There's nothing special about that! That's Uncle's son! I heard that his name is 'Hiro'! Look at him, he's gonna be just as great as Uncle when he grows up!"

Xiao Yu spoke up: "Sister, of course cousin Hiro is extraordinary! In this painting he is only one-month old, yet he already commands everyone's attention and adoration. Father painted him as the focal point to show the potential that Hiro possesses. But did you notice that darkened corner? That person in the corner? That's who I'm interested in!"

The children all looked towards the corner Xiao Yu referred to, only to let out a disappointed sigh.

"Sis! Are you crazy? That's just some old lady holding a baby boy. He's not even cute or handsome, and look how his frown wrinkles his forehead. What's so great about that?"

Xiao Yu looked sadly at the boy in the corner, her genteel manner showing already at such a tender age.

"Sister, that boy should be troubled. He's Uncle's adopted son!"

"What?" Chiu Hong got closer for a better look, but it just deepened her displeasure. "No wonder, look at him and you can tell he comes from base stock. No wonder they put him in the corner!"

"Sister, don't you think this boy is very special?"

"What? What's so special about him?"

"Father said that night was the first time he saw these two boys. You know Father is good at judging people by their eyes, after all he is an artist. He said that Uncle's son did not disappoint him, his eyes were brighter than all the adults there, and he will grow up to be someone great. But Father said the most unforgettable was the baby boy they left in the corner…"

"Even Father said that? He must be getting old…"

"No! Father said when he looked into the child's eyes, it was like feeling a thousand pounds pressing down on him. Father could barely breathe. He said that in all the years he's painted, he's never felt that kind of a gaze. It's like staring at a hero, you cannot bare to look directly into his eyes."

"Hero?" Chiu Hong said incredulously.

"Yeah! Father said that although the adults were afraid to look directly at that baby, Uncle's son stared at him all night, as if they were always brothers… Later, when the adopted boy looked back at Uncle's son, there was thunder and lightning in the sky. Father said it was like the heavens foretelling that these two boys would create a 'storm'…"

Before Xiao Yu could finish, Chiu Hong interrupted: "Okay, okay. Sis, I think that you've been possessed by this painting! It's just some pathetic abandoned baby; what's so heroic about that? You say Uncle's son stared at him all night and there was thunder and lightning? I'm just a child and even I don't believe in that story! Father must be making up stories to amuse you! Don't be so naïve!"

The other children also chimed in: "Yeah! Xiao Yu, don't stay cooped up here all day! We're playing house now, why don't you come play with us?"

Xiao Yu was in no mood to play. Her heart's attention had already drifted away… far away.

If nothing had happened to them, then the 'Hiro' and 'Hero' in the picture would be about ten years old.

What are these two amazing boys like now?

Hiro…

Hero…

Xiao Yu memorized the two names in her heart. She kept wondering what they were like. Would they possess the same light? What kind of storm will they bring?

That secret wish in her heart did not linger for long. One year later, her wish came true, and she finally had a chance to meet the two boys.

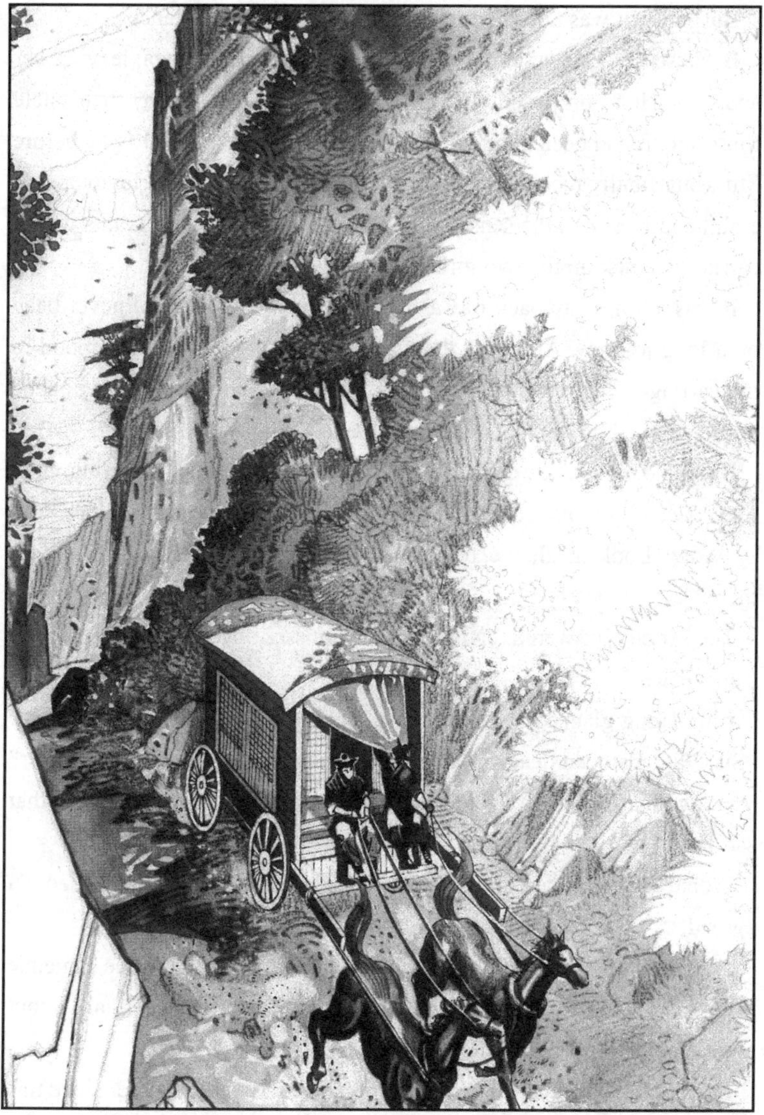

But sadly, it was not under the most desirable circumstance.

Because her Father suddenly passed away from influenza, leaving her and Chiu Hong orphaned. They were eventually taken in by their uncle Mu Long. It had been a month since Xiao Yu's father passed away before Mu Long finally received news of their father's death. As a famous general, he at least had the sense and obligation to send two servants with a carriage to pick up the two girls.

It was a long way back to Castle Mu. The two sisters had never been on a long journey. All along the way, Xiao Yu sat in a solitary mood in the carriage. The recent death of her father and her sudden move made her reticent.

But Xiao Yu's sister, Chiu Hong was especially excited about moving. She constantly looked out the windows, praising the country side.

"Wow! Look at all the beautiful scenery! How long before we get there?"

The servant answered: "Not long now, misses, just over that hill is Mu Long Town."

Chiu Hong glanced at Xiao Yu, and seeing her unhappy face she said: "Sis! Father's been dead for a month. You gonna look that way forever? We're gonna live with Uncle now; you'll make him miserable with that sad face!"

Probably the kindest thing Chiu Hong had ever said to her. Xiao Yu agreed.

"And don't forget," Chiu Hong continued, "we're going to see someone you really want to meet. Sis, remember you use to always talk about meeting Uncle's son and adopted son? Now's your chance!"

It was true! The chance was upon her! Xiao Yu still felt sad, since this chance came at the cost of her father's death.

The servant heard Chiu Hong's lecture.

"Misses, you wanted to meet Master Mu Long's two sons? You are arriving just in time."

Just in time? That piqued the interest of Chiu Hong and Xiao Yu and they listened intently.

"Yes, what a coincidence! If we can make it to Castle Mu today, it will be the same day young second master comes home"

"Comes home?" Chiu Hong asked with curiosity. "The young second master you're referring to is Uncle's adopted son right? What do you mean comes home? Is he not allowed to go home normally?"

The servant answered: "So you haven't heard about him? Of course, no wonder you want to meet him! If you knew about him, maybe you would feel differently!"

Xiao Yu anxiously asked: "Excuse me sir, but what's the matter with him?"

"Well, he's... he's a lone star!"

"Lone Star?" Xiao Yu asked curiously. Temporarily setting aside her grief over her father's death, she seemed especially interested in the fate of Mu Long's adopted son.

"Yes, even though Master Mu adopted him, he doesn't treat him nearly as well as his own son, even though Madame Mu insists on it. She felt that one must listen to one's own conscience, so Master Mu ended up going along with her. When we found young Second Master, he had a jade pendant with the words 'Hero' carved on it. Probably his irresponsible parents picked that as his name. However, Master's son was already named 'Hiro,' so to prevent confusion, Master changed his adopted son's name to 'Ying Ming'?

Irresponsible parents? Xiao Yu didn't think so. They named their child Hero, at least one of the parents must have expected great things of him. Especially the boy's mother, it must have been heart breaking for her to give away her own flesh and blood.

The servant continued. "Perhaps that child is really cursed! Madame Mu has always been very kind and even hired a nanny to care for him. But half a month later, the nanny suddenly died. Madame Mu hired another nanny, yet a few days after their one-month celebration, that nanny passed in her sleep. All of a sudden, we were all gripped with fear…"

"Why were all the servants afraid?"

"Well, he somehow managed to kill off two nannies; he just seems cursed. Maybe it would get around to one of us? Some of the serving girls even said that maybe the boy's bad luck even killed his own parents, and that's why he was abandoned…"

"But still, Madame Mu didn't believe it. She said it's sad enough he was abandoned by his parents, now no one wants to care for him. She decided she would breast-feed and care for him herself!"

Hearing that, Xiao Yu thought her aunt was really great to do such a kind deeds.

"But Madame Mu had always been frail. She already had to breast feed the young master Hiro, and then she had to do the same for the second young master. It was just too much for her. Finally she became gravely ill. The Master found another nanny to care for his son. As for his adopted son, there was no one else willing, so he was fed goat's milk."

"After the incident, Master deeply believed that his adopted son was bad luck. He began to distance himself and passed him around the servants, for them to care for him. Finally one time, the Master invited a travelling fortuneteller to stop by. When that fortuneteller saw young Second Master, it was like he saw the devil himself. He bolted out the door without a word. Master chased after him to find out what was wrong, and the fortuneteller explained on shaky legs that he had been telling fortunes all his life, but had never seen a child with such an omen. He said that the child was born as a 'Lone Star,' that it was his fate to hurt all those close to him; and that there was only one way for the Mu family to continue: get rid of him!"

Xiao Yu thought the fortuneteller's words were too harsh. "That's all superstition right? Did Uncle believe him?"

"Well, Master sort of half-believed. But Madame was adamant, perhaps she really grew to love him from the time she spent caring for him. She felt that his eyes were so kind, that he could grow up to be a good man and a great husband. She wouldn't allow him to be abandoned again, so she begged the Master not to heed the fortuneteller. Though Master was a stout-hearted general, he was still moved by his own wife's tears and her wasting away with worry. He finally thought of a solution..."

"What did he do?" Even Chiu Hong became interested in the story.

"Well, Master spoke at length with the fortuneteller. The fortuneteller said if he really didn't want to get rid of young Second Master, perhaps there was another way. If we could send young Second Master away some place with a harder life, it might wash away some of his 'unluckiness'. And when he came back to normal again, he could be brought back. This way it would protect the Mu family. But more importantly it will protect Master Mu's real son, Hiro. Since they were born on the same day, Hiro was especially affected by young Second Master's bad luck. Young Second Master must be sent away for eleven years, until his air of misfortune passed. Master Hiro would also be eleven by then, and would have strength enough ward off any bad luck. Even now, we must be careful, lest his bad luck returns…"

Xiao Yu is just a little girl, but she thinks their fear is a little ridiculous. Adults can be so blind sometimes. They can be more naïve than a child, more simply led…

She felt nothing but sadness for Madame Mu, who treated this abandoned child as her own, only to be separated from him… But, Xiao Yu's sister Chiu Hong seemed to believe the servant's tale.

"So today is the day he's suppose to come back?"

"Yes! That's right, it's been eleven years today, he's been gone. He's coming back today! Don't know if it's just a coincidence or fate! Anyway, Master found some martial artists to train young Second Master. But all of his teachers died within a year. Still, Master never allowed young Second Master to come home; he kept finding him new teachers. In these eleven years some of his teacher died of illness, others were killed. He's probably gone through seven or eight different teachers. Although they're not famous teachers by any means, I think young Second Master's probably now learned a hodgepodge of skills. He should be on par with young Master Hiro."

"But, I think Master doesn't like Ying Ming too much. Although he's coming home today, Master doesn't have anyone out to pick him up. Madame has tried to persuade him, but master said that a man has to live like a man; he shouldn't need anyone to wait on him hand and foot. If he has to be picked up, then he doesn't need to come home! But young

Second Master's last teacher lived in Yu Province--that's almost a thousand miles away. How can an eleven year old child walk all that way? It's too much if you ask me…"

Xiao Yu wholeheartedly agreed! Master Mu sent a carriage for the two of them, yet he was so cold towards his adopted son.

Thinking of the adopted boy Ying Ming arriving home today, Xiao Yu's heart began to beat faster.

If the eleven year old Ying Ming is really so extraordinary as to walk a thousand miles home alone, then Xiao Yu wants to meet him even more. The boy who's bad luck had killed off two nannies, eight teachers, and scared off fortuneteller… What could this boy like?

Thinking this, Xiao Yu lapsed into silence. Chiu Hong's further conversation with the servants went unheard, as Xiao Yu looked out the window toward the hill. Once over that hill, she will meet them, Hiro and Ying Ming at Castle Mu, a place that will effect the rest of her life…

Wrapped in deep thought, Xiao Yu suddenly heard a loud scream outside as an object was tossed inside the carriage.

With natural agility, Xiao Yu dodged the object, but it struck Chiu Hong squarely. The object landed as the girls leaned in for a closer look! They both were shocked to find….

The bloody head of the servant!

"AHHH!"

Chiu Hong was covered with blood from the severed head. She fainted immediately.

The usually gentle Xiao Yu was a little braver, and she did not faint. But Perhaps unconsciousness would have been better than those dead eyes staring up at her...

Just as Chiu Hong fainted, the carriage was splintered apart with a loud crack. Fortunately the girls were uninjured.

In the falling debris, Xiao Yu saw two men standing before her. Two savage, scarred men brandishing knives!

Bandits!

"Ah, you…you're…" Xiao Yu attempted to speak despite the grim situation. She held her fainted sister in her arms, trying hard to protect her.

The elder of the two bandits wore a cloth mask covered in blood.

"No more talking!" one said with an evil laugh. "Now that you've met the 'Two Scarred Bandits,' your life is over! Hey brother, check to see if they have any valuables!"

The younger of the bandits picked up his bloody knife and began rummaging through carriage. After a frantic search, he found nothing of value.

"Brother! You won't believe this, but there's nothing in this fancy carriage! There's only a couple of silvers."

"What!" The elder bandit was not pleased, looking down at Xiao Yu, he grinned.

"You're too careless in your search brother. Look at this girl, she's 'fair' enough' In a few years, she's going to be a bona fide beauty! A gem in her own right."

"You're right! Let's take her back with us. In a few years, we can sell her away, or we can sell her now to the 'Wang Butcher' for his meat dumplings. Hahaha, come with us, little girl…"

With that, the bandit reached out to grab Xiao Yu. In a panic, Xiao Yu bit down with all her might into the bandit's hand.

"AHH!! You little bitch, I'm gonna get you!" He reached out and

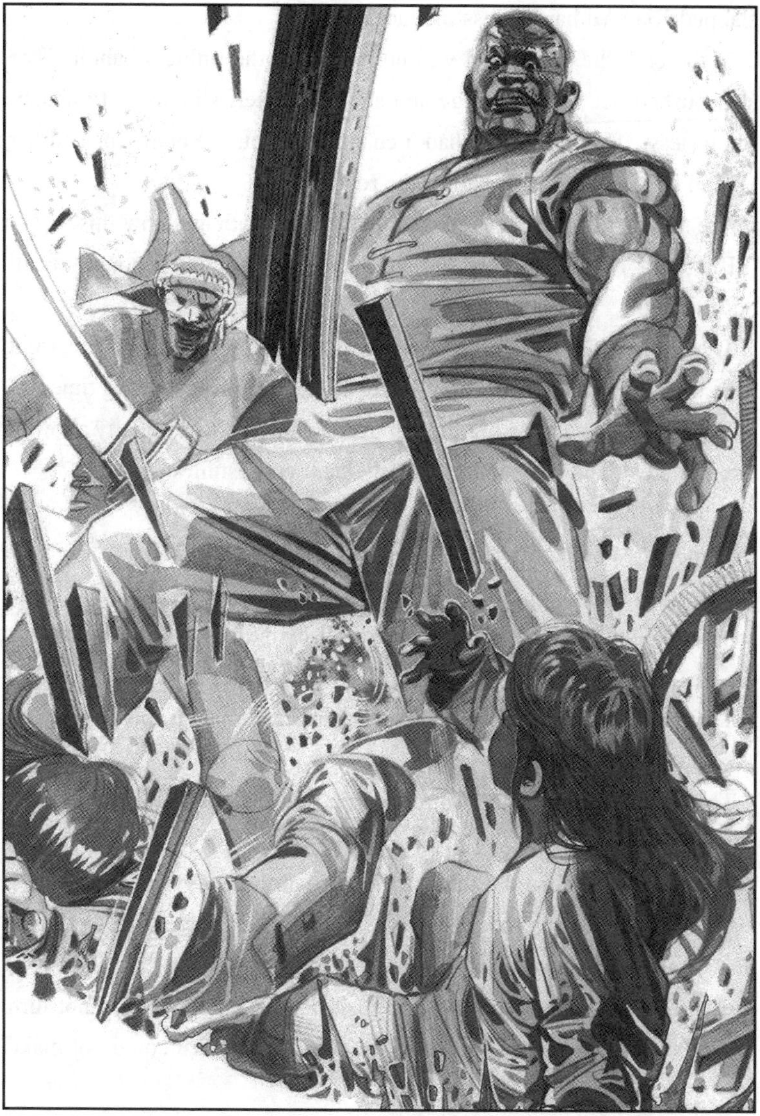

slapped Xiao Yu hard across the face.

In the end, the young girl was no match for the ruthless bandits. The slap pushed her over the edge and she felt herself slipping into unconsciousness...But before she had a chance to faint, the bandit picked her up and began carrying her down the road!

Are they really kidnapping her? Her father's death and now this?

But Xiao Yu had no more strength left in her, not even enough to call out for help.

The world is full of surprises, someone she's waited for all her life, right here, right now finally appears! Someone she has waited a long time for, but who will cause her a life time of heartache... Fate has finally allowed them to meet, and has begun to intertwine their destinies...

Xiao Yu, near fainting, vaguely heard the bandit yell out.

"Who dares block my road?"

After that the bandit fell silent, because he could speak no more. At the same moment, Xiao Yu felt a breeze waft by. No! Not just a breeze! A breeze, and... A "stance" within it! Just a single offensive stance!

Then the bandits fell silent! They stopped dead in their tracks!

Everything stopped!

The bandit holding Xiao Yu moved no more; she's finally saved! But who saved her?

The moment before she fainted, Xiao Yu struggled to open her heavy eyelids. The breeze had passed, as if afraid to linger. She wishes to at least thank her savior. And Xiao Yu faintly saw, in that breeze, a solitary figure! A boy with long hair, wearing plain clothes! The boy did not turn around to look at her. Despite her best efforts, Xiao Yu could not make out his features.

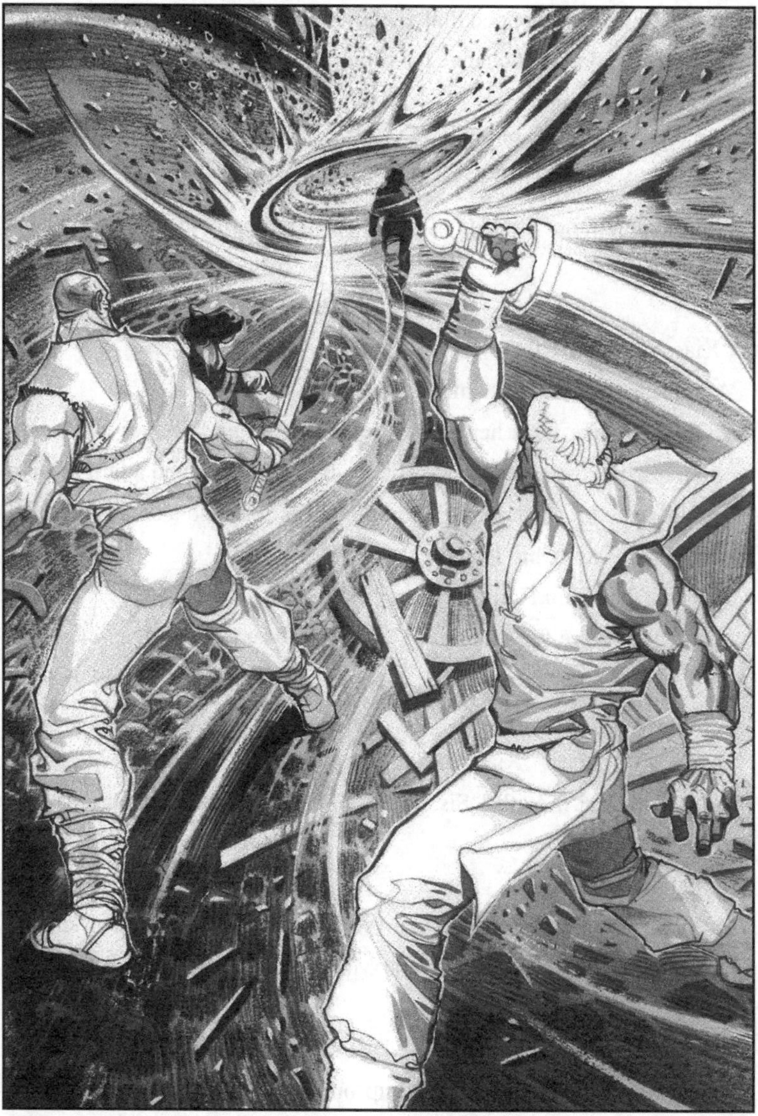

It's as if he never stopped, only helping her while passing by.

Meeting her does not change his solitary life. He saved her then moved on, solitary once more.

In his grand but lonely life, he is only accompanied by the breeze. Who is he?

Xiao Yu could not think any further, she had finally drifted into unconsciousness.

"Xiao Yu! Xiao Yu!'

A voice called out her name, urgently, but gently.

Xiao Yu awoke from her deep sleep. She opened her eyes and saw a comely middle-aged lady sitting at the edge of her bed and a tall, muscular middle-aged man standing behind her. There is also a small figure by her side, her sister Chiu Hong.

It seems that Chiu Hong recovered first.

"Xiao Yu, you're finally awake?" The lady beamed with happiness and gently dabbed away the sweat on Xiao Yu's forehead. Xiao Yu found herself in a luxurious bedroom.

"You… You are…" Xiao Yu felt groggy still.

Chiu Hong cut in with: "Sis, you don't need to guess. Meet your aunt and uncle?"

"Uncle? Aunt?"

As if waking from a dream, Xiao Yu knew this lady must be Madame Mu and the man, her uncle, General Mu Long.

"Xiao Yu, we're terribly sorry!" Madame Mu exclaimed kindly. "It's all because we didn't come pick you up ourselves that you met with such danger. Thank goodness it's all over now--but our servant, he…"

With that she began to sigh. Xiao Yu finally got a good look at the woman. Not only beautiful, she was also kind and gentle.

As for her Uncle, Mu Long, he stood silently brooding, like a lounging lion.

Chiu Hong cut in again: "Yes, the servant, he died! Luckily, Uncle and Auntie were worried and sent someone to look for us. They found us both unconscious on the hill in front of Mu Long Town."

Xiao Yu suddenly thought of something.

"Then what about those bandits? What happened to them?"

"Don't worry," Madame Mu replied, "when we found you, someone had already sealed their pressure points. They were defenseless and easily apprehended. They've been taken away to the local magistrate for sentencing."

Xiao Yu continued: "But… where is that other person?"

Madame Mu was baffled.

"What other person?"

"The one... who saved us."

The silent Mu Long finally spoke up.

"Xiao Yu, do you know who saved you?"

Under her uncle's fierce glance, Xiao Yu stammered; "No, after my sister fainted, I lost consciousness shortly after. I didn't see very clearly who saved us. I was able to catch a faint glimpse; he seemed like… a young boy!"

The words seemed to shock Mu Long.

"Im…impossible!" he grumbled, shaking his head. "How could it be a young boy who saved you? Madame, you know the "Two Scarred

Bandits" are the most notorious group of thieves in this region. Both brothers know a ruthless style of knife fighting that can split apart an entire horse carriage. They are famous for their martial arts. How can a boy, in a second, close all their pressure points? And don't forget, when they were questioned, they claimed they didn't see who did this. They said that a breeze blew by, and next thing they knew, all their pressure points had been sealed…"

As he spoke, he glanced at Xiao Yu.

"If, as Xiao Yu said, there was a young boy who did this, then he is incredible. Within these hundred miles, there is only one such boy…"

Before Mu Long could finish, a calm and confident voice chimed in from outside the chambers.

"Me. Right?"

All heads turned towards the door. Xiao Yu's face registered shock.

"Ah! Him! That's him… The one who saved me!"

The speaker stepped into the room. It was a young boy. Long hair framed his handsome face. He had a lean and lithe frame, just like Xiao Yu's savior. But when Xiao Yu finally saw the boy's face clearly, she realized that she had made a mistake.

Although she was only able to see her savior's back, she felt that boy had a sense of infinite sorrow about him. This boy in front of her looked similar, but the feeling he instilled was completely different!

The boy in front of her exhibited a bright and energetic face. A face that bespoke a confidence and elegance; a ruler, "a ruler of swords"… Not only was his voice confident, he seemed even more so in composure.

When this boy looked at Xiao Yu, it was as though he could look into her heart, a feat he performs on everyone he meets. Xiao Yu could not meet that confident glance. Embarrassed, she lowered her gaze.

The boy turned up a smile and said: "Cousin Xiao Yu, are you sure, the one who saved you was me?" His tone was far more mature than his age of eleven might suggest.

Cousin? He called Xiao Yu cousin? Doesn't that make him... Xiao Yu immediately realized who was speaking to her, but her sister was even quicker,

"You're...Cousin Hiro?"

Yes, this was General Mu Long and his wife's only birth son, Hiro! Is this the boy predicted by Sword Saint to one day become the ruler of swords?

"Oh! No wonder! You're just as great as your father here! So heroic and brave!" Chiu Hong began spouting all the flattering phrases she knew of. Sometimes not even realizing what she was saying.

But when Hiro heard them, his smile disappeared; he turned to face Chiu Hong.

"Shut up! How dare you call me your cousin! Aside from my parents, no one is allowed to call me by title. You're calling me cousin. Are you trying to imply that we have some relation? I don't care who you are... Do you think you are worthy enough to call me that?"

Chiu Hong was shocked! She could not believe that an 11-year-old boy could be so arrogant. She knew that she had made a mistake and quieted.

Madame Mu was also shocked; she has been around Hiro all his life. He had always treated everyone with respect. Today was the first time she had ever heard her son speak this way. She quickly tried to smooth things over.

"Hiro, don't be so rude to Chiu Hong. You should be respectful to all your relatives."

Seeing the proud air his son displays, Mu Long secretly took pride.

"Madame, this is not so. A man should always seek to be better than others. He should strive to be the best!"

Seeing her husband protect their son, Madame Mu was at a loss for words. Hiro turned back to Xiao Yu and the smile returned to his face. He seemed more interested and respectful of her, much more so than towards Chiu Hong. He asks: "Cousin Xiao Yu, let me ask you once more. Are you really sure that the one who saved you is me?"

Facing her cousin she's always wanted to meet, she did not feel disappointed in the slightest.

"No," She politely responded, "I think that I have mistaken you for someone else. You're not him, but you look so alike…"

Before she could finish, Hiro rushed ahead.

"He looked a great deal like me?"

"Yes."

"If we look so much alike, how do you know I am not the one?"

"Well, " Xiao Yu began, "Although I didn't get a good look at his face, for some reason he seemed… so sad. And Hiro, you're so…"

She did not know how to describe her confidently smiling cousin! Hiro answered for her.

"I am overly arrogant? Prideful?"

Xiao Yu was shocked that he could criticize himself without any hint of shame! In that moment, Hiro released her from his penetrating stare. He turned toward his father smiling and said: "Father, looks like sister Xiao Yu met another boy who saved her who is the same age and looks as I do. You've been teaching me all my life; I'm confident that I could handle the

'Two Scarred Bandits' without a problem. But there's another boy around who can defeat them as well? Isn't that interesting?"

"I wish I could meet this boy!"

As he spoke, a challenging gleam flashed in his eyes.

Mu Long was silent, pondering the same thing. With his fearsome "Mu Family Palms" he was able to rise through the ranks. He was probably among the top ten fighters in the land. Who else could have a boy to rival the skill of his own son?

A series of urgent footsteps sounded outside the chambers, as a servant rushed in.

"Master! Madame!"

Seeing the fearful look on the servant's face, Mu Long turned to him.

"What's the matter? What do you have to say?"

Stammering, the servant said: "Master! It's terrible, the dogs guarding the front are barking incessantly!"

"What? Why are they barking? Who are they barking at?"

"They're barking..." the servant in his hurried voice could barely get the words out. "They're barking at young Second Master!"

Young Second Master? Was that the unlucky adopted son? He's made it back home alone, without any assistance?

Hearing the news, Xiao Yu's eyes lit up with eagerness. Madame Mu heard the news with delight, and Mu Long's son Hiro, also had a gleam in his eyes.

Only Mu Long frowned. He thought that he had made a wise decision, swapping his real son for an adopted son. But who knew that he brought home such an unlucky child. Rubbing his beard, he thought "He's finally back? He came back all the way alone. He is pretty tough! I thought he wouldn't be able to make it, an 11-year-old boy and all--but he did it. Incredible..."

Mu Long turned to the servant.

"Then why are the beasts barking at him?"

"I don't know sire! I was just ushering young Second Master into the front room, when all the dogs started barking madly. They were barking and retreating, as if they were afraid that young Second Master might 'bad luck' them to death..."

The servant clamped a hand over his mouth. He knew he said something wrong.

Luckily Mu Long didn't catch it, and replied: "Madame, Ying Ming is back now, we should go see him. Hiro, Chiu Hong, why don't you two come along! Xiao Yu, you've just woken up, why don't you rest a little longer and recover."

Xiao Yu had been dying to meet Ying Ming face to face, but now her Uncle had forbidden her to come. Secretly she was filled with disappointment, yet just as everyone was heading out the door, Hiro stayed behind. He turned towards Xiao Yu.

"You really want to see my brother?"

Xiao Yu blushed, and lowered her head.

"Brother Hiro, I don't know what you're speaking of."

"Really?" Hiro's eyes measured her and looked into her heart.

With a joking tone he said: "Girls are so much trouble! They want it, but they pretend so hard not to want it!"

"Like me, I would never be like that. Honestly, he's been gone ever since we were little; I've not seen him since. I wonder what he looks like?"

"If as father says, his bad luck killed off two nannies and eight teachers, then he must be pretty incredible! Such an exciting younger brother, I am eager to meet him!"

It is apparent that he is not afraid of his brother's bad luck. Just the opposite, he seems excited and intrigued by it.

"You really don't want to see him?" He repeated his question to Xiao Yu.

"I…" Xiao Yu didn't know how to respond.

With another smile, Hiro said: "It's okay! Father told you to get some more rest, but you seem pretty rested to me. I think that you want to come along. Follow me!"

With that, Hiro dragged Xiao Yu up and carried her out hurriedly.

"Brother Hiro…"

Disregarding his father's command, Hiro bravely brought Xiao Yu along to go see his "infamous" brother!

Isn't this the moment she'd been waiting for?

The boy holding her, Hiro, in every aspect--from speech, thought to looks, was like an overconfident "alien creature" to her.

But an alien creature that did not disappoint her!

What about Ying Ming, will she be disappointed to meet him?

Perhaps he is a creature more alien than Hiro!

He always has his head down.

The servants are all staring at him, talking under their breath, as if watching some strange creature. The ten guard dogs, with their tails between their legs have retreated to a corner.

A hero never bows down, and one who bows down is not a hero.

Why does he bow his head down?

The Hero Bows

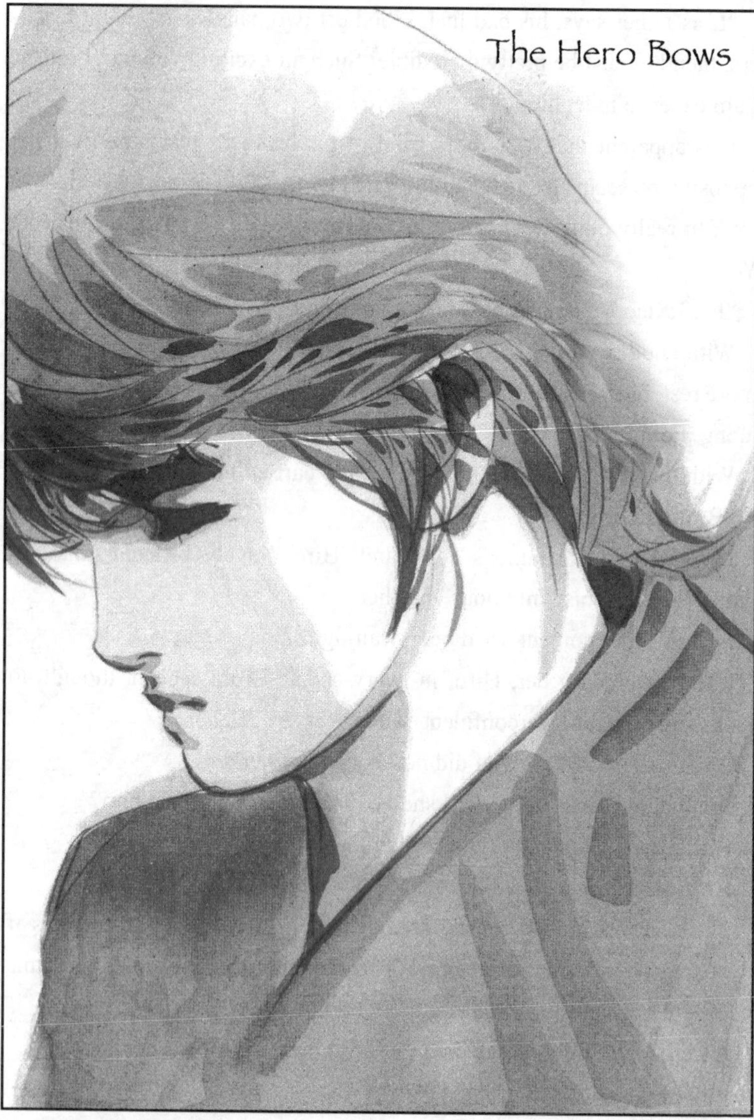

When Mu Long, his wife and Chiu Hong rushed to the front room, they saw him with his head down.

A bowing Hero!

He is eleven years old, wearing plain black clothes covered with grime from the road. In his left hand, he clutches tightly a small bundle. As if fearful of ruining the upscale furniture, he sits in a small dark corner of the room. But the front room is too opulent; there is no where to hide. The contrast is too great, like a single thorn among a flawless bed of roses.

The servants stared from afar, no one wanted to approach him. Even the dogs cowered in fear of the strange guest.

The first glance of this sorry figure huddle in the corner filled General Mu Long with disgust. Chiu Hong followed on his heels like a obedient dog. She shared his sentiment, and also discriminated against him.

But Madame Mu's eyes rimmed with tears upon seeing this poor child. She exclaimed with excitement: "Ying Ming? Are you Ying Ming?"

Everyone avoided the boy, even the dogs, yet Madame Mu did not hesitate to welcome him. Sadly, no one saw his look of gratitude.

"Ying Ming. Mother has missed you... so much!"

Madame Mu rushed forward, and disregarding protocol, held him by the shoulders. Everyone avoided touching his dirty clothes, yet Madame Mu was not afraid to dirty her expensive silk robes. She was happy to see him.

"I can't believe... that you're so... big now! Do you remember... when you were still very... very small... I held you in my arms. You looked up at me with your little eyes filled with fear, as if everyone would abandon you. Since that time, I knew, although you are not my real son, I will always love you as my second-born. I wanted to take care of you always, but…"

An unconditional love! Madame Mu already loved this boy with all her heart, perhaps because of her kind nature, or she just saw something in the boy no one else noticed. Although not blood related, they were mother and son by fate, and nothing escapes fate…

Traditionally, the men in Chinese households had the final say. No matter how much she was against it, she could not prevent him from being sent away to such a harsh life…

Kindly, she asked: "You've been away for so long, how have you been these 11-years?"

But looking at his tattered, dirt-stained small hands, and shabby little cloth pack, it was apparent how he had fared alone for so long.

Seeing Madame Mu's eyes fill with sad tears, the boy named Ying Ming seemed touched. He didn't want her to feel so sad, and the normal taciturn boy nodded his head gravely and said: "I am fine. Don't worry, Mother."

He finally spoke! Two short, unforgettable phrases. His speech was slow and sullen, not at all like a normal child's. But his tone was filled with a warmth; he was not cold, at least towards Madame Mu.

Though Madame Mu had treated him warmly, he did not give an overwhelming response, as if trying to keep a distance from everyone. Perhaps because he felt that no one would want to come near him, so he put up a barrier.

Madame Mu found that Ying Ming's voice sounded very much like Hiro's.

Shaking her head, she said: "You're a such a thoughtful child, you didn't want Mother to worry about you. You don't have to lie to me. I know that you've had to switch teachers eight times. You've never had a place to call home. It must have been terribly tough for you. But don't worry now, because Mother will make it all up to you. You don't have to live this way any longer. Castle Mu will be your final home. Do you understand?"

He understood completely. Sometimes in life there are partings that can not be avoided. After eleven years of wandering, he well understood the sorrows of life more than she could know.

When Mu Long first adopted this boy, it was based on Advisor Bao's cunning strategy. Mu Long thought to use the boy to replace his real son in battle. So he never told his wife that the boy was their neighbor Autumn's son. And he never could have predicted, the son he bought, would be such an unlucky one.

He never would have thought, that after intentionally making the boy's life hard, and not sending anyone to pick him up, that the boy would make it home all alone. What more, he couldn't imagine his wife would treat this boy as her real son. He was angered more than he would admit.

"That's right!" he interrupted. "Castle Mu will be his home. However, it depends on his suitability to live here. Madame, just look at him, your kind words are completely wasted on him. He hasn't even looked at you. His head has been lowered all this time. Look at him clutching that dirty pack. Is what's inside that pack more important than your greeting?"

Madame Mu just realized that Ying Ming never looked at her during their entire exchange. Still she did not mind, and tried to defend him regardless.

"It's not like that, Master! It's been a long road home, I think that Ying Ming is just tired. Ying Ming! Here, let me hold your pack, why don't you go rest in your room?"

She reached out for the pack but her adopted son held on, with no intention of giving it up to anyone.

Madame Mu worried but understood he might not be use to someone else helping him, but Mu Long was greatly angered.

"How dare you! What are you hiding in that old, crummy pack of yours? Open it now!"

Sensing her husband's rising anger, Madame Mu tried to quell the situation.

"Long, there's nothing special about a child's pack. It's just a child's stuff in there! Allow him some privacy!"

"Madame," Mu Long insisted, "you will spoil him with your leniency. I know you are a gentle woman and don't want to discipline your children, but he's not your real son! Besides, if you really want what's best for him, you should strictly discipline him."

Standing to the side, Chiu Hong continued to look down on Ying Ming. In her heart, she thought this boy was like dirt compared to Mu Long's real son. Seeing her uncle's displeasure, she was quick to take sides.

"Yeah, Uncle is right! Actually, we children shouldn't have any secrets at all. Ying Ming's pack couldn't have anything that important!"

Chiu Hong's taunts provoked no reaction. With his head bowed down, Ying Ming gravely responded: "Mother, should not look at the contents of this pack." His tone was even lower than before, to the point of extreme humbleness.

His answer merely mystified Mu Long more. Chiu Hong tried to get further into Mu Long's good graces,

"Ha! There's nothing that auntie can see in there! Let me see it!"

With that, she reached for Ying Ming's pack. Somehow the pack suddenly slipped out of her hands. His hand was incredibly fast!

Though he is fast, he is not as fast as the powerful Mu Long!

Mu Long shifted to the side and stretch out his fingers like talons. With one swoop, he ripped the bag from Ying Ming's hands and through it against the floor. With a loud clatter, the contents of the pack were strewn across the floor. Mu Long's face turned livid when he looked closely at the items.

Inside the pack were numerous "funereal plaques"*. The plaques scattered across the floor in a bizarre and macabre scene.

*(*Editor's Note: It is customary in China to create carved wooden plaques of respected family elders or masters who have passed away. Usually the plaques are adorned only with a carved name and honorific title in respect. These plaques are kept as a way to honor ancestors, as ancestor worship was common in ancient China.*)

Seeing the contents, Mu Long seethed.

"You little bastard! How dare you bring these evil omens to my home? Are you trying to curse my whole family?"

With that he stomped down on the pile of plaques, breaking and shattering many in the process.

"No…" The normally silent Ying Ming gave out a low scream.

"Don't destroy them!"

He ran behind Mu Long and firmly latched on to Mu Long's leg.

Now angered beyond belief, Mu Long yelled: "You want to stop me? You can't!"

Planning to kick him aside, Mu Long was shocked to find he could not move his leg at all. He thought to himself "Where is he getting this

123

strength? I have been practicing martial arts for decades, and this mere boy has strength enough to subdue me?"

Just as he was planning to forcefully kick Ying Ming aside, Madame Mu stepped in.

"Long! Please, I beg you! Look!"

Mu Long glanced in the direction Madame Mu pointed. On each of the plaques was inscribed with the letters "Respectfully to my Honored Master."

Madame Mu looked towards Ying Ming in sadness, tears already falling.

"My child, these eight plaques are of the masters that raised you these past eleven years. You don't want to forget them; that is why you have brought them home. You want to respect and honor their spirits in heaven, is that right?"

Ying Ming bowed his head, but made no reply.

Madame Mu was touched.

"That's right! Everything they have done for you deserves to be remembered and honored. Your eight masters must have been especially kind to you…"

Yes, in the small boy's mind, scenes from the past eleven years assailed him…

His first eight masters were not from any great school or sect. None of them had anything extraordinary to teach. Yet each made an effort to raise this "lone star" that was so easily tossed away by Mu Long. The first time that each of the teachers laid eyes on him, they knew he was a martial arts genius.

Though they were each ordinary, they tried to pave the way for his future--a future of legend. They had all heard about his unlucky nature, but willingly accepted his burden...

In the end, each of these masters died. Was it merely coincidence, or was it truly a curse the child possessed?

Madame Mu continued: "Each person who has helped us, deserves a special place. My child, if your masters knew that you had carried them on this journey home, they would be so honored. I am sure that they are smiling down on you from heaven..."

Madame Mu's heart went out to her young son. Alone he carried these plaques for a thousand miles, not losing or damaging a single one. Now her husband cruelly disrespects them. Yet there was still one last thing she didn't understand.

"My child! If these are your honored master's plaques, why did you say that I shouldn't see them?"

Ying Ming didn't answer. He merely stared sadly at the ruined plaques, perhaps he did not wish to explain.

Just then, in the moment of silence, a loud voice rang out.

"I know why he doesn't want Mother to see those plaques. It's probably because he knows that Mother's birthday is coming up soon!"

The speaker's voice bares a strong semblance to Ying Ming's. It's Hiro!

Amidst the commotion, he had silently arrived with Xiao Yu!

Him, him, and her... They finally meet. Their complex relationship had now finally begun...

Hearing Hiro's explanation, Madame Mu was thrilled. Turning back to Ying Ming, she asked: "My child, is it really because of my birthday? You thought that seeing something associated with death on my birthday

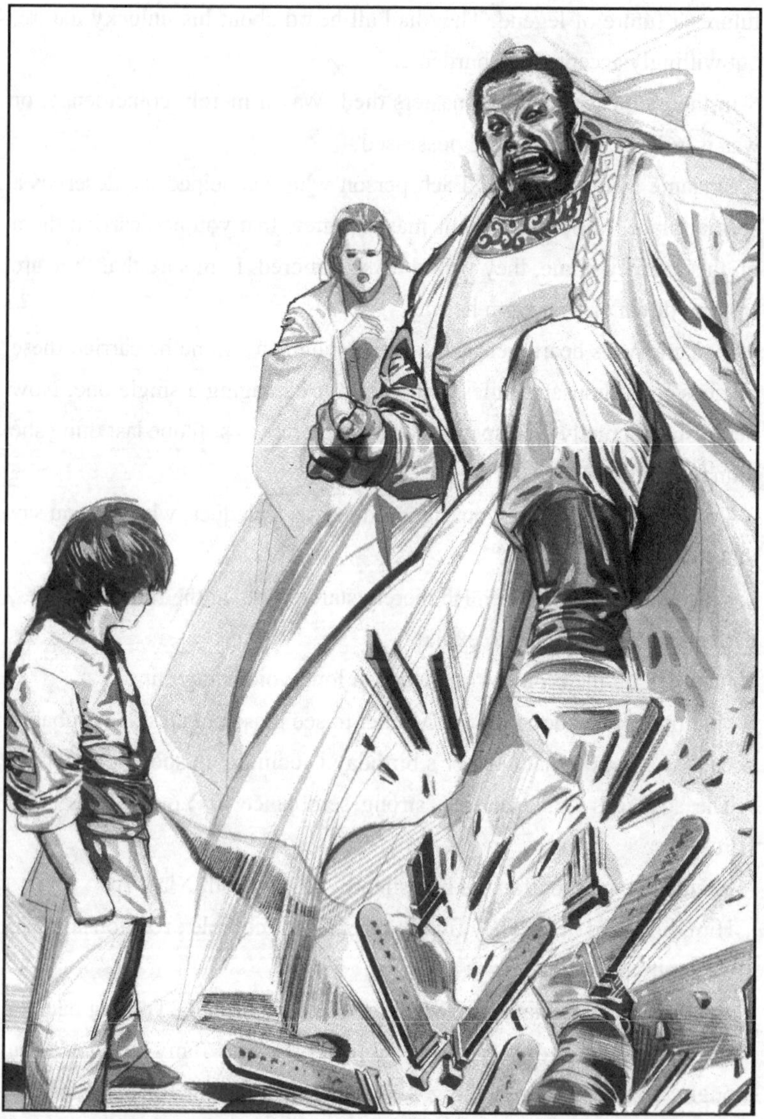

might've brought bad luck?"

Ying Ming did not nod or shake his head, but the truth was evident. Thinking of his thoughtfulness brought another tear to her eye.

"My son, you are so silly. You know I've never been one to believe in these omens. I've never believed in bad luck..."

It's true! If not, she would not have treated this boy like a real son. She never believed in fate! She only believed in a clean conscience! The conscience of a devoted mother...

"On yes, I haven't introduced you yet. Look, this is your older brother Hiro! This is your cousin Chiu Hong! And this beautiful girl here is your other cousin Xiao Yu!"

Xiao Yu had been standing in the room for some time. She had been most anxious to meet both Hiro and Ying Ming. Immediately she thought him somewhat strange with his head always bowed. Hearing her aunt describe her as a beauty, she blushed with embarrassment.

Although, Madame Mu enthusiastically introduced each person to Ying Ming, he still never looked up. The hero's head still down.

Xiao Yu was disappointed, because she still had not seen Ying Ming's face. This especially angered Chiu Hong. She felt that in his eyes, she didn't even merit a glance. As for Hiro, he merely smiled; he seemed to find his younger brother very interesting.

One anomaly usually finds another amusing!

Initially feeling shameful over destroying the master's plaques, Mu Long's anger rose once more with Ying Ming continued silence.

"Ying Ming! Your mother is making introductions for you, why won't you lift up your head? I want you to look up now!"

Even Mu Long's order was not enough to bend his will. He continued looking down.

Mu Long was a general used to having his orders obeyed. In battle, his command decided the lives of thousands, and here was this young child, daring to defy him. He was furious.

"If you don't do it now, I will kill you right here!"

Ying Ming remained unmoving, which incited Mu Long further! Just as he brought his hands up, Madame Mu rushed forward to stop him. At the same time, Hiro suddenly spoke up.

"Father! Are you raising an obedient dog?"

Mu Long's palm stopped in midair.

Mu Long has always doted on his son Hiro. Now that his own son had voiced dissent, he didn't know what to say.

"Hiro, you…"

Hiro's eyes shone with a bright wisdom uncommon to children his age.

"Father," he began, "if Ying Ming really did raise his head like an obedient dog, then I wouldn't like him very much! He is your adopted son after all! If he was obedient like a dog, doesn't that make me a dog's brother? And you father of a dog? That makes us a whole family of cowardly dogs!"

Hiro deftly averted the disaster! With a few simple words, Hiro was able to diffuse the situation. Mu Long was shocked, but also pleased, with his son's intelligence.

"But, Hiro, as you know, he is a lone star. His bad luck has already killed off two nannies and eight teachers. And today, he's brought home eight funeral plaques. He even has this incurable habit of always looking down!"

"Really?" Hiro said, smiling at Ying Ming. "It's truly unfair that you think of him as a lone star! Those two nannies were quite old already, it's natural that they should pass away in their old age. As for his teachers, they were too ordinary to achieve more fame with martial arts. It doesn't prove that he is a lone star. Lone star implies a lack of confidence in one's own destiny. It's just some superstition invented by the uneducated…"

Hiro's reasoning left no room for Mu Long to interject. Madame Mu cheered in her heart. She for one has never believed in the whole lone star thing.

And Xiao Yu, she had originally thought her cousin Hiro was overly confident. Now hearing his eloquent defense, she thought him deserving of all his confidence!

As for Ying Ming…

Hiro had defended his long held title of lone star, but he didn't seem to react--his body shaking ever so slightly.

Even such a slight movement could not escape Hiro's eyes, the eyes of a ruler! Seeing Ying Ming's body move, Hiro's lips turned up slightly.

He smiled.

This was Hiro and Xiao Yu's first meeting with Ying Ming. Yet he always kept his head down. Although they could not see his face, they could never imagine that this boy would grow up to be…

A hero whose fate intertwined with theirs!

A hero they will never ever regret meeting!

After that incident, Mu Long began to see Ying Ming as a thorn in his side and treated him accordingly. But in the end, he abided by the wish of his son and wife, and did not force Ying Ming to lift his head. He simply ordered Ying Ming to leave the funeral plaques outside the antechamber. Those plaques that had been damaged, he merely threw away!

Life is a game, filled with many limitations and many rules. Even a hero must follow the rules, if he wants to survive.

From that day onward, Castle Mu had some new guests, two girls and one boy.

A hero who always bows his head.

No one knows why he does so.

No one can make him do otherwise.

The bowing hero continued bowing, and those who thought him weird, continued to think him weird.

In the blink of an eye, eight days had passed. Ying Ming had been living in Castle Mu for eight days. And none knew how Ying Ming spent these eight days. Since the first day he stepped into Castle Mu, he remained secluded and reclusive.

To show her affection for Ying Ming, everyday, Madame Mu would get up extra early, rub the sleep from her eyes, and go into the kitchen to heat a vat of water. Then, unaided by her servants, she would carry a basin of hot water, for washing, into Ying Ming's room. As wife of the master of the castle, she could order any of her hundreds of servants to do these menial tasks. Yet she insisted on doing them herself; she wanted to show her son that she really did love him. But after the first two day, she could no longer find him in the morning. But each day she continued to lovingly bring the basin of water to his room.

He got up earlier than Madame Mu? Was it because he felt ashamed? Perhaps he was afraid that his bad luck would rub off on others? Or did he feel unworthy of her great love, and was avoiding her? Was he just letting himself go?

Madame never gave up; she still got up everyday and brought hot water to him, rain or shine.

Although Ying Ming was never in his room during the day, Madame Mu cleaned it for him. Sometimes when she saw the clothes he was wearing were worn, she would sew them herself. Of course, it would have been easier for her to buy a brand new outfit for him, but she knew a mother's hard work was always better appreciated…

There were somethings in this world that money could not buy…

Madame Mu had done everything a mother could do for her son. Aside from having a clean conscience, she was also grateful for his thoughtful behavior in trying to conceal the plaques from her in fear that they were unlucky. That was enough to make her think that she had a wonderfully caring son. Since Ying Ming's return, Madame Mu had put all her heart into caring for him, even neglecting her own son. Yet Hiro never resented it at all.

He always smiled confidently at everything.

Perhaps a confident person had no need for jealousy. Or perhaps he knew that the love his mother gave would be returned.

On the night of the fourth day, Madame Mu began to bring water to Ying Ming; she returned to her bed chamber to find two basins of hot water placed square on the night table ready for her and Mu Long to use.

Mu Long did not wonder where the water came from--after all he had plenty of servants to see to his needs. Only Madame Mu knew… She knew who prepared the water.

Because she never was in the habit of washing her face before bed, so she would never have had her servants prepare something like that. She knew it was "someone" returning a favor…

Although "he" never personally thanked her, she knew quite clearly…

Just like that, every morning Ying Ming's room would have a basin of hot water, waiting for a lonely child to use, waiting to provide him warmth and love. As if to tell him that no matter how much the world turned against him, one woman, would always love him as a mother…

And every night, in Mu Long and Madame Mu's bed-chamber, there would be two basins of hot water, returning the wordless love of a kind mother…

Mother and son continued to maintain this secret. Madame Mu rarely saw Ying Ming in Castle Mu.

Castle Mu was truly grand. It would not be hard if someone wanted to hide away in some corner. Even if the Castle were to be searched, it would take an entire day and night.

So no one saw Ying Ming, it was like he had disappeared.

Every lunch and dinner, the Mu family would gather around and enjoy a meal together. Mu Long, Madame Mu, Hiro, even Chiu Hong and Xiao Yu attended. But Ying Ming was always missing. He might be getting food directly from the kitchens.

Since returning home, why was he avoiding everyone? Was it because he knew that Mu Long thought he was an unlucky omen. Eating with the family would only anger his father. He would rather bear the unhappiness alone.

Perhaps because he knew too much of sorrow?

Not only Madame Mu, but Mu Long, Xiao Yu, Hiro, Chiu Hong and all the servants in the household never saw him in those eight days. Since the first day he arrived with his head down, no one had been able to see his face clearly.

What kind of person was he? Was he handsome? Ugly? Everyone wondered. Especially Xiao Yu, since long ago, she had imagined this boy abandoned by his birth parents countless times.

Though, his whereabouts had been mysterious, she still had a chance to see him.

It was on the eighth day of his return… That night, Xiao Yu walked towards Ying Ming's room with a package. It was late into the night, yet Ying Ming was still no where to be seen. Xiao Yu couldn't help but feel a little disappointed. It was getting late, Xiao Yu began to worry,

"Ying Ming… where did you go? It's so late already, and he is just a boy; he should be in bed asleep now. He…"

Thinking of her own situation, she quickly amended, "Xiao Yu! You're also up late, so of course, he might be up as well. Perhaps, there's something important Ying Ming is doing?"

The impropriety of her waiting in his room so late into the night suddenly dawned on her. She decided to try again tomorrow. Following the path along the garden, she passed by the kitchen. There she heard a strange sound!

It was a series of scraping sounds, not at all associated with cooking.

Xiao Yu grew curious and tiptoed towards the kitchen. Castle Mu's kitchen was extremely large. When Xiao Yu walked in, she saw someone sitting in a darkened corner, someone she has been waiting to see: Ying Ming!

Ying Ming had his head bowed down, a serious mood pervaded his demeanor. By his side was a nearly spent candle. He held a piece of wood, and there looked to be similar pieces lying across the floor. Concentrating, he carved away on the wooden blocks. Seeing someone enter, he quickly hid the blocks under the stove.

In that brief instant, Xiao Yu caught the words Ying Ming carved on the wood, it said "For My Honored Master!"

Ying Ming didn't look up, he knew that she had seen them. Breaking his usual silence he said, "You found out."

Yes, Xiao Yu finally found out. Mu Long would not let Ying Ming keep any plaques inside the Castle. Directly in defiance, he had been carving new plaques for his eight deceased masters. Did these eight masters really treat him so well, that he was risking everything for these little honorary symbols?

This is Xiao Yu's first time alone with him. The usually silent Ying Ming spoke up to her first, which was pleasantly shocking to her. Hearing the tone of his voice, she feared he would misunderstand.

"No! Brother… Ying Ming. I didn't do it on purpose! I… was planning to bring something to…you. But since I couldn't find you, I was going to try tomorrow. I passed here on my way back; it wasn't on purpose. Don't worry, I won't tell uncle!"

Her voice urgently tried to convince him of the truth of her words. Ying Ming understood, but only numbly replies, "You don't need to cover up for me. Why are you doing that?"

His question made Xiao Yu blush, and stammering she answered, "Brother… Ying Ming, you want… very much to honor your masters, even at the risk of offending… uncle. Your masters… would be proud to have a…. disciple like you…"

He said nothing.

"Well, it's getting quite late! Brother Ying Ming, I… should be going back to my room. Don't worry though, I won't tell anyone…"

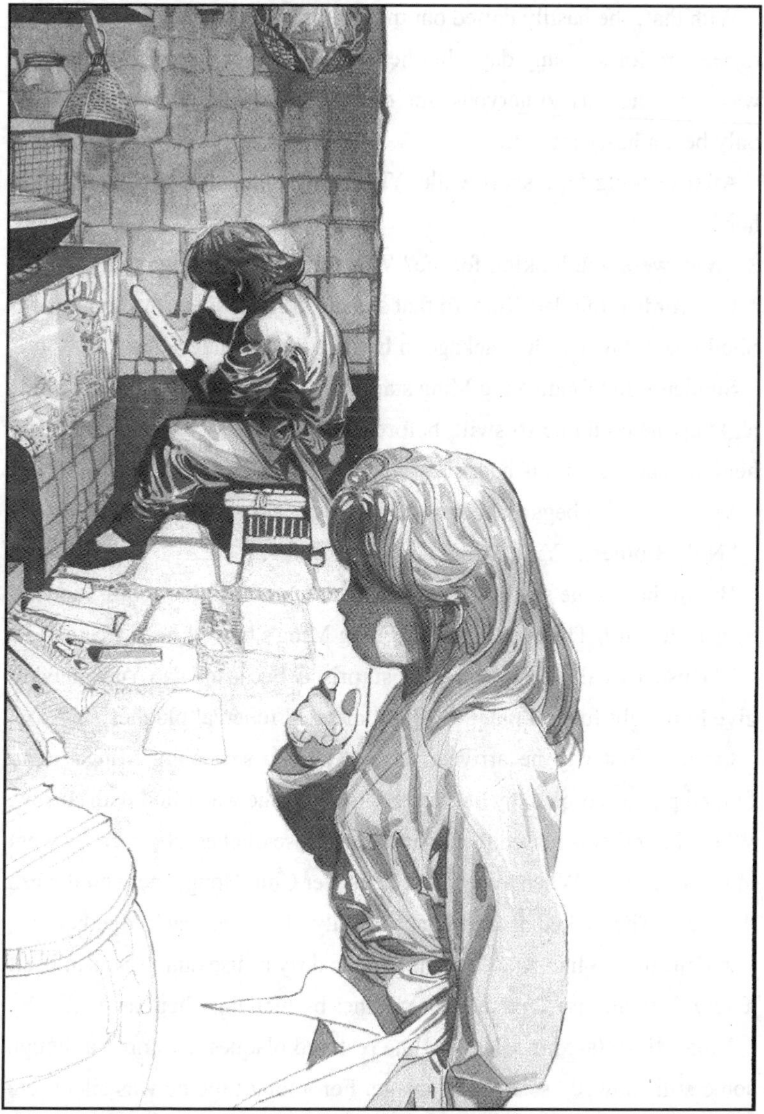

With that, she hastily darted out the doors. When she had been wanting to see him for so many days, but he was never to be found. Now that he was here, she was so nervous, she did not know what to say. She could only beat a hasty retreat.

After walking for a short while, Ying Ming suddenly called out to stop her.

"Why were you looking for me? What did you want to give me?"

His words reminded Xiao Yu that she did come to give him something. She looked down at the package in her hands with indecision.

Suddenly she found Ying Ming standing close behind her. Xiao Yu didn't know he could be so swift, before she even had a chance, Ying Ming held the package in his hands!

Wordlessly, he began opening the package. Xiao Yu panicked.

"No! Brother... Ying Ming, don't look at it..."

But in the end he saw it. His hands were faster than her words, and his eyes faster still. The contents made Ying Ming's bowed head shake.

The usually calm Ying Ming was surprised, because Xiao Yu wanted to give him eight funeral plaques! Eight mended funereal plaques!

On that first day he arrived, when Xiao Yu saw Ying Ming's eight funeral plaques broken by her uncle Mu Long, she was filled with sorrow. When the servants tossed them out in the refuse ditches, she secretly went to retrieve them. When away from her sister Chiu Hong, she would wash the pieces she picked up and then carefully glue them back together.

A delicate girl like Xiao Yu going to the dirty refuse dumps was in itself a very difficult task; but she went further by mending them as well!

Ying Ming stared in silence at the restored plaques. Restored although some still showed "scars" of damage. For a long time he was silent, but finally he spoke.

"Why did you do this? You didn't have to."

Xiao Yu's face turned red with embarrassment, and biting her lip, shyly she replied, "Because I was returning the favor... a favor to the person who rescued me from the bandits."

Ying Ming seemed shocked, but did not ask anything further. Xiao Yu continued.

"Although I did not see my rescuer, and I haven't seen your face yet, I feel that it was you. There is that same sense of sorrow about you…"

Ying Ming denied it.

"Perhaps, you remember wrongly… You should only ever trust your own eyes, and never your feelings… I am a useless, unlucky person."

"Really?" Xiao Yu seemed slightly disappointed with Ying Ming's denials, but she persisted. "But that person had enough strength to rescue me from the bandits. If he really was merely an eleven year-old boy who had been under the tutelage of a group of patient yet lowly masters, he still had the skills to stop both bandits. That boy must be someone special; he should not give up on himself, he should never…"

She paused.

"Bow down his head! A hero does not bow. Brother Ying Ming, I heard that before my uncle renamed you, your birth parents gave you the name…. 'Hero'. Don't let it be in vain…"

Xiao Yu spoke as much as she could, and although she knew he would never admit to rescuing her, she still tried to encourage him as much as possible.

Yet, Ying Ming remained unmoved. With head still held low, he says, "Yes! I use to be called Hero, but... now I am Ying Ming."

"To be a hero is a tiring thing."

"That's right!

Being a hero is lonely! Being a hero is suffering!

Every age in history is filled with glorious heroes. Yet in the end, they are washed away in the tides of time.

"To be a hero is to be much more than ordinary!"

Ying Ming realized this truth at such a young age. His wisdom shows a sense of his lone star philosophy. Xiao Yu did not know how to respond, and just then Ying Ming diverted the topic.

"If you've found my master's plaques, why didn't you show me?"

Shyly, Xiao Yu answered.

"I... just saw the ones you carved. I thought the new ones you've made looked so good. And mine... are just the ones I made from broken pieces, they have... lots of chips and lines... They're so ugly... I just felt that...I didn't really do such a great job, so... I didn't want to show you..."

Ying Ming looked at the eight chipped plaques, and suddenly packed them gently into the package, slinging it across his shoulder, and tossing the new plaques into the stove.

"Brother..." Xiao Yu exclaimed, "Ying Ming, why are you... burning your plaques?"

Not looking at her, Ying Ming merely walked out of the kitchen, but he didn't forget to leave her with one more thing,

"I think that if my masters in heaven knew... they would feel that the ones you patiently mended, are prettier than the new ones I made."

Really? Is that true? Or perhaps he appreciates the thought this girl put in.

Regardless, he walked away, without saying any more...

Xiao Yu stared at his retreating figure, her eyes filled with regret.

It was sad that someone with so much potential was doomed to feel so useless and melancholy.

Sadly...

Yes! It is truly sad! Even Madame Mu felt the same sense of regret...

Late into the night, Madame Mu awoke from a dream to find her husband Mu Long had fallen asleep at his desk. But at sometime during the night, somehow he had been covered by his cape. Madame Mu clearly remembered that before she went to bed, she had not put the cape on her husband. Her husband would never think to do so himself, then who covered him?

Being an expert martial artist, it was not easy to sneak up on Mu Long. That person must be extremely fast and dexterous.

Madame Mu thought of someone: him. If he could really put the cape on her husband without waking him, then what is his true potential?

She thought of how hard her husband had been on him, yet he still tried to show respect to Mu Long. He had a generous heart. Yet Mu Long continued to treat him as something base and lesser.

None can do all that can be done,
Do what your conscience tells you.

The sun rises, but did not bring "him" hope. The sun sets, but did not bring him relief.

"He" continued to live mysteriously and numbly in Castle Mu.

Soon the rumors of a bowing "hero" spread to Mu Long Town and beyond.

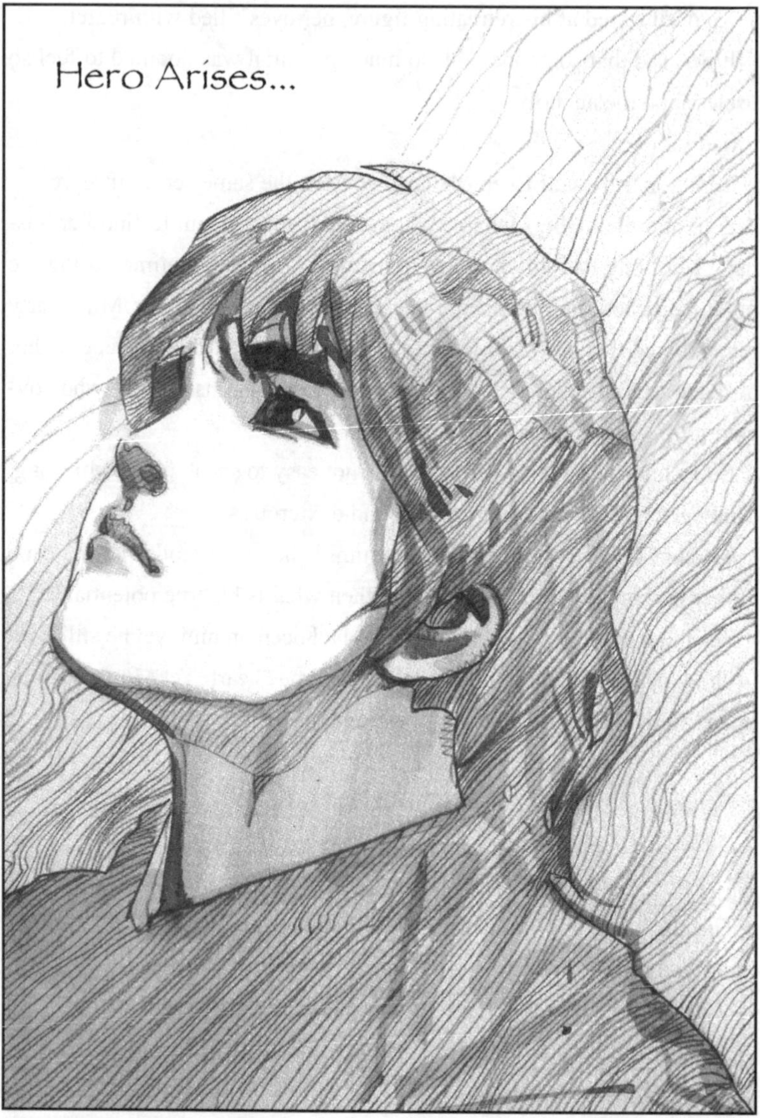
Hero Arises...

Everyone was curious, Mu Long was a famous general known for his bravery in battle. How could he have a son that never looked up? It seemed a very shameful matter! People always had an interest in the base deeds of the famous. In less than half a month, the story of Ying Ming and Hero became common knowledge.

Some people even went as far as lingering outside Castle Mu, hoping for a glimpse of this strange child, yet they were always disappointed.

Of course! Even those within the castle did not know of this child's whereabouts. Not even Mu Long.

Since this son's return, Mu Long had only seen him a few times. And when he did, he mocked his son, and berated him. He hated this child, this unlucky omen! This lone star!

And, as if to confirm everyone's suspicion, bad luck soon showed itself! Within half a month of his return, the vicious guard dogs of the castle, those that had barked at Ying Ming's presence, contracted the plague and perished. It was easy to associate their their death with Ying Ming!

The story of a bowing lone star grew until it was told in every street and every alley.

Sometimes, when the servants saw him from a distance walking in the Castle, they would scurry away in fear. Some of the younger girls, who saw his shadow approach would begin crying, fearing that death would soon be upon them.

The grand Castle Mu soon was wrapped in a cloud of superstition and fear...

But there were some who were not afraid.

Like Xiao Yu. She and Madame Mu both felt Ying Ming was not a lone star. All the unlucky thing happening had nothing to do with him.

Although Xiao Yu's sister, Chiu Hong, always urged her to avoid Ying Ming, whenever Xiao Yu passed him, she would always glance at him several times; though he always has his head bowed, and she never really could see his face.

As for Mu Long's son Hiro... Being so confident, he never tried to avoid Ying Ming, but neither did he try to approach sullen young boy either. Every time he met Ying Ming, he would just look at him with interest, as if looking at a heavenly statue of a "hero"! A statue as perfect as himself! Hiro's eyes always sparkled with light, and no one knew what he was thinking, just as no one knew what the lone star was thinking.

If Ying Ming is an oddity, then Hiro is one as well.

Madame Mu treated these two oddities equally. She was doing her best as a mother. Although one is not her real son, even if he were a beggar on the street, she would want to help him. Men should treat all equally, and she won't begrudge her own son, or Ying Ming.

She deeply believed that the deaths had nothing to do with Ying Ming; it was all just coincidental. If this child had really been cursed by the heavens as a lone star, then was that really unfair? She could never accept that a child who would prepare her wash water every night could be a lone star. And she would never believe that a child so thoughtful could kill his birth parents with his bad luck.

It's injustice! Because it's not fair, and Madame Mu treated this boy even better. She absolutely believed that if she would just show him kindness, he would grow to be a great man! She did not believe that a person could be born noble or base, and that a person should always live with his head bowed down. She knew that time would change how everyone saw Ying Ming! When all the unhappiness and death surrounding him faded away, people would forget, and they would no longer think of him as a lone star.

Madame Mu wanted time to prove everything; she thought she would have her entire lifetime to raise him as her son, but their days together were not long...

There were too many unjust things in the world.

Finally, one day, the unlucky fate of a lone star would fall on someone who had always believed in him!

And that someone was Madame Mu!

It was the 30th day of Ying Ming's stay in Castle Mu, and the day of Madame Mu's birthday banquet. Mu Long held a banquet for her in Castle Mu, inviting guests from far and wide. He did not want the thorn in his side, Ying Ming to attend, but Madame Mu insisted.

"Long, you know what I wish for the most is to see our family together. You've put together this lavish banquet for me and I am very grateful, but if Ying Ming does not come, what meaning will it hold for me? Long, if Ying Ming really was a bad person, I would know that he was beyond help. But you've seen how he's made the thousand-mile journey home alone. He's even carried along the plaques honoring his masters all this way. Such a sweet child, I want him to know the love of a mother. Since fate had made him our adopted son, we should treat him so."

Mu Long knew of his wife's affection for Ying Ming, and it was her birthday after all. He should let her have her way.

"Madame, since you insist, I won't go against your wishes! But I have to tell you, the fortuneteller said that he would be the death of all those close to him. If he appears at your birthday banquet, I am afraid that... I don't know what might happen..."

"Nothing will happen!" Madame insisted.

"Long, if Ying Ming really could kill those close to him, then just let it be. I don't believe it, and I wouldn't mind it. Ying Ming is a good boy, there are so many things he has done you don't know about…"

She wanted to tell him about the water he's been preparing for them, and the night he covered Mu Long with the cape, but Mu Long already grew impatient.

"Okay, enough Madame! I just want some peace and quiet now. I don't want to hear more about that irritating boy!"

With that he walked out of the chamber.

Madame Mu felt her husband unwavering in his views of Ying Ming. There was nothing she could say to change his mind. Right now all she could do was let Ying Ming know that she wanted him at her banquet.

She went to look for Ying Ming, but of course he was not in his room. She waited a long time, but he did not show, so she had to leave a note…

My child, tonight is your mother's birthday. Long will be holding a large banquet in the Castle for me. I would be very happy if you attended. If you could sit by Hiro next to me and we can all be together as a family, that would make me even happier. Don't let your father and those in the castle look down on you. I believe that you are not a lone star! I hope that you will lift up your head!

Her brief note told him of a mother's high hopes for him. She must want him to lift up his head and live his life not bowing down to fate. This note recorded the wishes of a kind mother, but will Ying Ming see it?

That night, when all the guests were gathered in the great hall, and

Madame Mu was pondering if Ying Ming would arrive, a small figure slowly walked toward the entrance.

The guests had begun to present their gifts to Madame Mu. As a general of high standing in the court, Mu Long had many noble guests. As long as he wished, many in the court would come at his bidding. Friends and family seeking his favor also arrived in drones, and the gifts they brought lined the hall in splendor and luxury.

Even the children all had gifts for Madame Mu.

Especially Chiu Hong and Xiao Yu. The sisters sewed a delicate handkerchief for their aunt. Seeing their beautiful work, Madame Mu was filled with happiness. And her son Hiro gave her a scroll of his calligraphy that wished her good health and longevity. Seeing the wonderfully written scroll, the guests were amazed that a child of eleven could produce such magnificent work. Hearing the praise of all the guests for her son, Madame Mu felt it was the best gift he could have given her.

All parents want their child to succeed.

She wanted not just her own son to succeed, but for her other son as well. She hoped to hear such praise for him as well, because she knew that he had suffered so much more, and received so little happiness...

And though Hiro brought Madame Mu glory, someone not so glorious, at that very moment approached the happy gathering!

Perhaps Mu Long felt the boy was not worthy, but Madame did not think so.

When he appeared, the hall fell silent. The laughter and boisterous conversation suddenly fell dead! And Mu Long's smile disappeared from his face!

Everything stopped!

All guests' eyes fell on him!

Because "he" was an unlucky person, he should not be appearing at such a happy place!

He should not! He was unworthy!

Ying Ming walked with purpose towards where Madame Mu sat. He walked slowly, each step a labored one; his every move weighted by the curiosity, prejudice, and fear of all the other guests.

If he knew he had to suffer their ridicule, why did he come? Was it because… He saw the note Madame Mu left? He wanted to fulfill her wish and not to allow them to look down on him. Despite his heavy steps, no matter how difficult, he still came!

He was wearing the old shirt he arrived in. Although the fabric was ordinary, it was clean and mended; but Mu Long felt ashamed nonetheless. This child's clothes were worse than those of the lowliest servant.

The guests stared with a mixture of curiosity and fear. In the past month, they had already heard about this unlucky lone star, and finally now they saw that, as rumor had it, he really kept his head bowed.

But Madame Mu did not look down on this son. Seeing Ying Ming walk towards her, she already beamed with happiness. The only thing disappointing her was that his head was still bowed down; he had not lifted his head as she had wished. That he attended though, was enough for her.

"Ying…Ming? You've really come?" She exclaimed, "I'm so happy! Come, come. Sit by your mother's side, let me introduce you to our friends and guests!"

With that, she swept her small disappointment aside and pulled Ying Ming to her side, bidding him to sit on her left, with Hiro sitting to her right.

"Everyone!" Madame Mu spoke with pride, "This is my second son Ying Ming! He and Hiro were born on the same day, and they even look alike! Especially their voice. It is very similar; my two sons were, perhaps, linked in a previous life!"

Alike? Linked?

Perhaps only Madame Mu thought so, but the gathered guests did not think Ying Ming and Hiro were so much alike.

In their eyes, one wore a robe of delicate silk, embroidered with silver and glistening in the light, like some prince from a fairy tale. The other was dressed in a plain, coarse robe, with head bowed, lowly and tattered. How could these two be alike?

There was no praise as Madame Mu had hoped for! No applause, only silence!

Even if none of the visiting guests agreed with her, there were two who did. Xiao Yu and Hiro.

They felt that the silent treatment given by the guests was excessive and rude. Hiro acted first by grabbing Ying Ming's arm and pulling him by his side, speaking loud enough to be heard by all.

"Yes, my mother is right! Even I think we look very much alike! Don't you all think so?"

Hiro laughed heartily as he spoke, his penetrating gaze piercing into each guest. With his glance came this unseen pressure, and then the guests, upon hearing Mu Long's own son praise the boy, agreed.

"Yes... Haha! The two of them are so alike... like twins!"

In an instant, the hall filled with laughter, and all signs of fear disappeared. Seeing her own son stand up for Ying Ming, touched Madame Mu. And Xiao Yu as well viewed Hiro in a new light. She thought to herself, "Well said, Cousin... Hiro, he is a good person!"

Amidst all the happy laughter in the hall, Ying Ming asked Hiro in a low voice, "Why do...you keep helping me?"

Hiro's lips turned up slightly forming a smile, speaking softly in Ying Ming's ear, he answered: "Because you're interesting! There are too many boring people in this world! Look all around at these guests; they are all mindless ants... Their exteriors may be grand, but it is just a facade, within is only emptiness. They are merely sucking up to the biggest ant, my father! And you..."

He looked at him intently.

"You are not an ant! You are different!"

Ying Ming seemed to stir, but he still did not lift his head.

"You like to keep your head bowed down, but when everyone looks down on you for doing so, you are not affected. You continue to do what you think is right, regardless of their accusatory glances. I don't think you have given up on yourself. Just the opposite, I think you are courageous! I know that there must be a reason you are doing this. And another reason I am helping you is for Mother! She really loves you very much, and is always trying her best to treat you with kindness. Mother doesn't care what other people think of her--she doesn't care about that--only wanting to do what she feels is right by her conscience. She is a good woman, always..."

Ying Ming and Hiro rarely meet, and rarely speak, but now Hiro has opened up to him. Hearing him describe their mother, Ying Ming felt the same.

"She is a good woman... a great woman."

Hiro smiled.

"Ying Ming, my brother, if Mother heard what you just said, she would be so happy! But if you want to make her happy now, just sit at the table and enjoy the banquet!"

Yes, it only takes her family sitting together around the table, to make this woman happy. Ying Ming knew this of course, and he sat down. But although the two brothers wanted nothing more than to make her happy, there were always troublesome elements wanting to stir up trouble.

"Yes, today is auntie's birthday. Cousin Ying Ming, did you bring a gift for her?" Chiu Hong suddenly asked. She was trying to make him look bad! Seeing his coarse clothing, it was apparent he did not bring anything.

Madame Mu didn't want to embarrass Ying Ming, and tried to explain.

"No, it's okay, it's okay. You're just a child, you don't need to give gifts…"

Before she could continue, Mu Long cut in.

"That's not true! Madame, all the children here have brought gifts for you. Ying Ming is a good child right, then he should have something for you. Ying Ming, where's your gift?"

He glanced at Ying Ming with a wicked grin.

It's hard to imagine a grown man mocking and stooping to this level to shame a small child. Hearing that Ying Ming silently reached inside his tunic to pull out an item. Squarely he delivered it into Madame Mu's palm.

Madame Mu looks closely, examining Ying Ming's gift…

The jade pendant his parents left him! It is the jade pendant carved with the words "Hero"…

But at the moment, beside the words "Hero" were carved four small words: For my beloved mother.

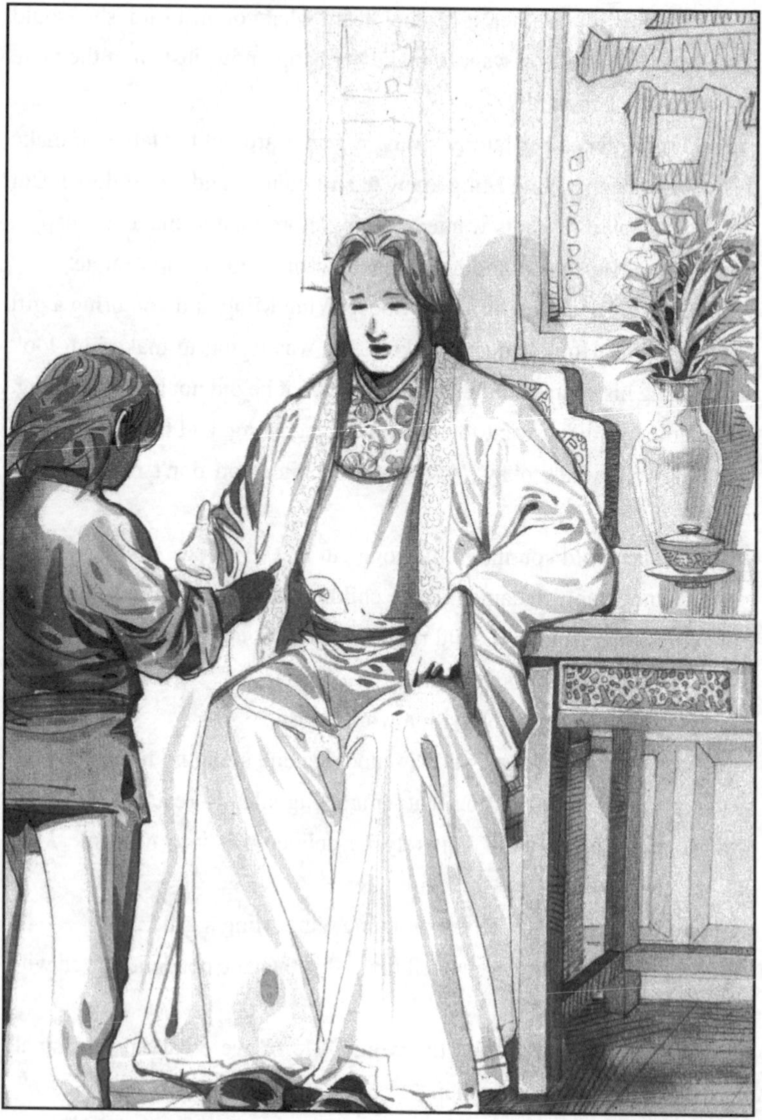

These small words looked newly carved. It was very apparent that Ying Ming carved them himself. He had given his only valued possession to Madame Mu. A gift from the heart, just as he might give to his true mother.

Madame Mu has always loved him from her heart, she has always been a kind woman. She never hoped to receive anything in return. Seeing Ying Ming give this jade pendant to her, she was shocked.

"No, Ying... Ming. This jade pendant is all that's left from your birth parents... how could I take this? I am not worthy of such an honor!"

She tried to return the pendant back to him, but he would not take it. He did not look at her, as if trying to tell her that she was worthy!

Although they have only been together for a short month, no matter where, no matter when, she had always protected and loved him, treating him as her real son!

Seeing his insistence, Madame Mu is deeply touched. She knew that if she continued to refuse, he might misunderstand her intentions. He might feel that she did not want this pendant. In order not to hurt this fragile child's feelings, she accepted the pendant and with care hung it above her breasts. But just then Chiu Hong spoke up,

"Auntie, that jade pendant is so old and ugly! It's not really valuable, you don't need to pretend it's that important!"

Madame Mu was usually very patient, but hearing Chiu Hong continue to embarrass and insult Ying Ming, she could no longer contain her anger.

"Chiu Hong, you are still young, you don't understand what this means to me! Do you realize that this jade pendant is more valuable to me than all the gold and jewels in this hall?"

"Because it was given to me by someone I love and have the highest hope for! I hope that the son who gave this pendant to me will become the "hero" carved here--a great man who will live up to this hope!"

Her tone was a bit heavy and serious. The guests felt insulted that she liked the old jade pedant better than their more expensive gifts. Madame Mu did not care how they felt, she just gently held Ying Ming's arms, full of happiness.

"Ying Ming, I know this comes from your heart. I will temporarily keep this pendant for you. It is your only link to your birth parents, and I can not take it for my own. When you grow up, I will give this back to you fully intact..."

She still did not want to take this away from him. She knew whoever carved the words "hero" on the pendant must have wanted him to wear it, hoping to protect the child, and help him become a hero one day...

As a parent, she could understand the hopes of another parent.

Because she understands, she could not accept this gift, this pendant of great import...

Still she accepted the gift to show her appreciation for Ying Ming, and to give him face in front of so many guests. Mu Long looked at the boy with more and more anger, feeling that he had to bring this banquet to a close before any more embarrassment occurred.

"All right! Since we're all here now, let's begin the banquet! Enjoy!"

The guests began to feast, but just at that moment a cold voice rang out from outside the gates of the castle.

"A feast! Mu Long, you dog! You have made enough to last a lifetime, this feast is proof. Mu Long, I have come to avenge my father's death!"

With that, ten swords speared through the doorway, quick as lightning.

The guests began to flee in fear.

"Ahh, it's an assassin! Assassins!"

Cold steel glistened in the light! Mu Long in his climb to be a decorated general, had made many enemies! An assassin was nothing unusual for a man of his standing!

A general, who had seen many battles, Mu Long calmly faced the ten swords slashing towards him.

"Cowards, how dare you come during my wife's birthday banquet! Get out!"

He lifted his left palm and struck, turning the swords back towards the direction from which they came.

The guests were amazed by General Mu's martial arts ability. But the ten swords did not find the targets they were intended for, because outside were ten great swordsman!

In an instant, ten shadowy figures rushed into the great hall. Not only that, but some twenty more swordsmen followed closely behind. It looked like a well-planned attempt. Every one of the assassins wore a mask and black clothing. One particular tall man stood out, with a silver dragon sewn on his clothing, apparently their leader.

"Mu Long, you dog! You are as good as they say! The first ten of us will take you down, while the other twenty will kidnap your wife!"

With the command, the assassins launched their attack! Hearing their plan, Mu Long knew the first ten attackers were probably better than the others, but with the attacks focused on him, there was very little he could do.

Although the other twenty assassins were not as skilled as the first, they were still quite fearsome. Like a pack of hungry wolves, they descended upon Madame Mu. Madame Mu sat clutching the pendant Ying Ming just gave her. She had no skill in the martial arts, so there was little she could do!

In an instant, twenty swords surrounded her, a man with a purplish masked laughed.

"Hehe! You bitch, your husband has done too many bad deeds, but his kung fu is too good. Today I, "Purple Crow," along with my clan brothers under our leader "Little Dragon King," will capture you. Don't resist, or you will get hurt!"

So the man with the silver dragon is their leader: Little Dragon King?

Purple Crow stretched out his right hand like a claw, and was about to seize Madame Mu, but a angry voice rang out like thunder.

"I will stop any who dare to hurt my mother!"

Suddenly Purple Crow screamed, for a sword had just lopped off his right hand!

It was no ordinary sword!

And its wielder was no ordinary person!

Hiro! He's revealed his skill!

The assassins all froze with shock! The guests were even more amazed! Everyone knew that Mu Long's son had been under his father's strict tutelage, but none knew his true ability. With a sword in his hand, he exuded a ruler's mien! His attack was decisive and quick!

However, the assassins were highly trained, even with his hand cut off, Purple Crow had enough sense to press the pressure points to stop the bleeding, and issue orders to the other assassins.

"Don't be scared! We'll split up, ten of you continue attacking that bitch and the rest of us work on that dog's bastard son!"

"Bastard?" Hiro laughed coldly, "No one calls me bastard! You will pay for that!" With that he swung his sword to claim his prize.

Prize? Purple Crow had already paid, with his right hand! This time he was a bit wiser, he bellowed a single powerful command.

"Guard!"

The remaining assassins jumped forward and blocked as one!

Although Hiro had the chi of a ruler of swords, he was still a young boy. With his father under heavy attack, he fought alone and his strike was deflected.

Having nineteen people block the attack of one boy did not seem so glorious, but the assassins were only after victory, so they did not care about their methods. The men surrounded Hiro. They were no ordinary martial artists; Hiro's situation began to worsen!

Seeing his own son surrounded, Mu Long worried. But he himself was pinned down by ten strong assassins. Their leader, "Little Dragon King" was especially formidable. He could not afford to be distracted, and as much as he wanted to help his son, there was little he could do!

Another ten rounds passed as Hiro began to grow tired. Yet his eyes still blazed with the same light and his ruler's chi did not lessen. He fought with all his might!

More important, under the barrage of attacks, he could not circulate his chi properly. Just when his chi seemed to weaken, eight swords broke through his defense. Attacking from all directions, they headed towards Hiro. Is this the end for the Ruler of Swords?

No! Because the least likely person, the one no one could predict, finally attacked! His martial arts skills are finally revealed, so that he may save Hiro!

The eight swords came towards the confident Hiro. Although he remained calm, he knew he didn't have a chance. He could have never predicted that in that moment before death a sword would strike out like lightening, blasting down on the eight swords attacking him. It stabbed into the ground next to Hiro, shattering the eight swords to pieces.

What mysterious sword saved the young Master? How could it cut through the eight swords as if they were mere clay?

Everyone looked in amazement, and were shocked to discover that the sword they saw shattering the eight swords, was nothing but an illusion! It was no sword at all, but a person, a person filled with sword chi! The chi of swords surrounded him, giving him the appearance of a sword!

His skill shocked everyone in the hall. Mainly, because he too was only eleven years of age. Without a single weapon he charged into battle. With one stance, he broke eight swords and negated the assault!

This sword-like person was the ever-bowing Ying Ming! Hero!

With the eight swords broken, Ying Ming broke through the attack and stood by Hiro guarding.Yet he still held his head low, not giving the assassins a single glance. This person seemed like a sword destined to shine in battle!

A natural born sword, a heaven sword! A sword that shined with the glory of battle!

Hiro possessing the chi of the ruler of swords seemed slightly dim in comparison!

Those in the hall no longer looked down on him for not lifting his head. They were filled with shock! The most stunned seemed to be Mu Long! All these years, he found low level masters for this child. He didn't think the child would ever amount to anything! He didn't need for them to train

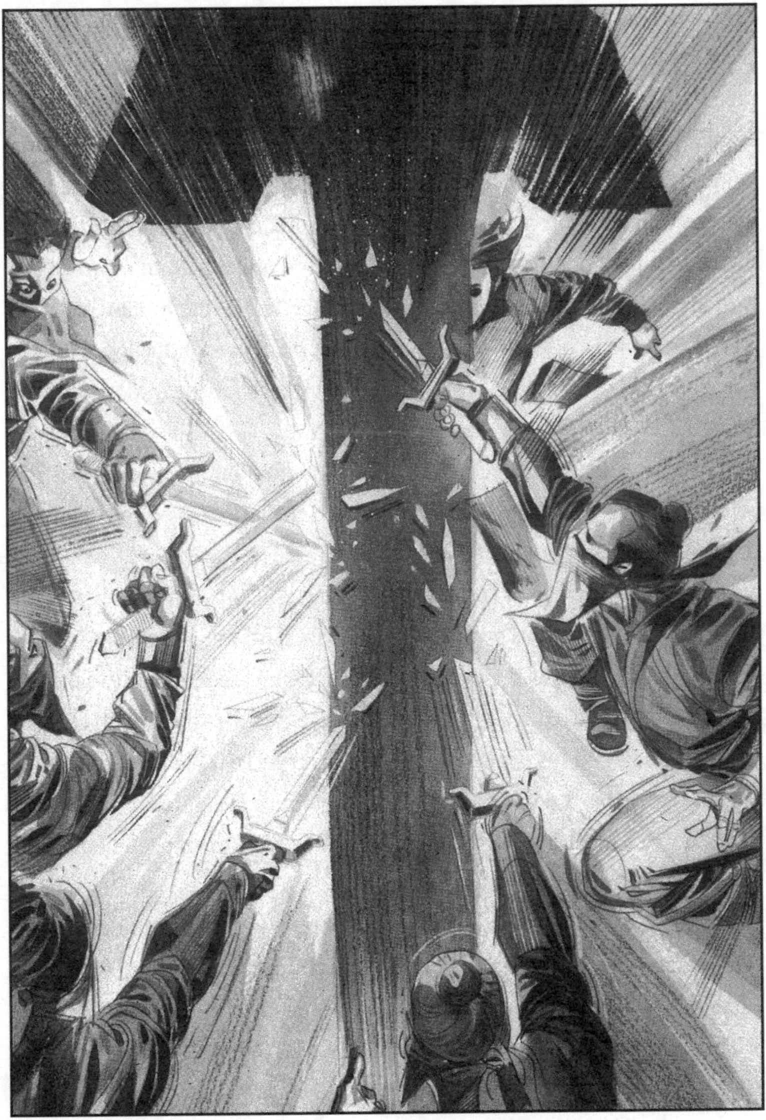

his "lesser" to be a good martial artist. His sole purpose was to take Hiro's place, battle and die by Sword Saint's hand. He could never have imagined that under the tutelage of such lowly skilled masters, he could defeat eight highly trained assassins! This display of skill was on par with Hiro, who had been under his father's direct tutelage! How could those ordinary masters train such a student! Perhaps that student was truly gifted and blessed by the gods! He was a natural warrior, and a natural swordsman!

Madame Mu was especially mystified. She knew that her adopted son was no ordinary boy, he was just self-depreciating. But why, with his uncanny skills, was there reason for him to keep his head down all the time?

Hiro was especially shocked! He felt all along that his brother was not so simple, but he would have never known that Ying Ming might be stronger than he! With his help, Hiro was rescued.

Only Xiao Yu was not surprised! She' had always known. Her rescuer who stopped the bandits with one stance that day was Ying Ming!

Purple Crow seeing the prowess of Mu Long's second son was taken aback. Always the calculating one, Crow assessed the situation. It seemed that Mu Long and his sons had enough power to beat back the assassins, but the mission must accomplish something! He looked around at Madame Mu beaming with happiness at her son's unexpected show of skill, and a plan formed.

If they could not kill their target, they could kill someone that would effect the target and his sons. The Mu family must pay with blood! Mu Long has committed many atrocious crimes in his rise to power.

The purpose of this assassination was to take the life of Mu Long. The leader, Little Dragon King, had planned on using Madame Mu as a hostage to force Mu Long to commit suicide and avenge his father, who died unjustly by Mu Long's hand. Little Dragon King would never kill Madame Mu; he was not interested in the death of innocents. He only wanted to kill the one responsible.

But Purple Crow did not agree. He looked at Madame Mu coldly and with his remaining left hand, he picked up a sword on the ground and leapt into the air, stabbing towards Madame Mu!

His attack met no resistance. Without his right hand, all thought he was incapacitated. No one suspected that he would attack. The sword struck directly toward Madame Mu's throat!

"Madame!" Mu Long has always truly loved his wife. Seeing her in such peril, he desperately wanted to help, but could not.

"Purple Crow, we are not here to harm women and children! Stop!" But it was too late!

"Auntie!" Xiao Yu and Chiu Hong screamed, but their shock was not as great as Hiro's!

"Mother!" Hiro roared, and the confident air disappeared from his face, replaced by a look of morbid desperation! Disregarding his own safety, he burst forth out of the attacking circle, five swords scratching across his body. But he didn't care; he just wanted to save his mother!

He had always been arrogant, but he was a good child!

However, although Hiro was quick, there was someone quicker!

Someone like a sword!

A figure darted out of the circle of blades like a sword of lightning! A lightning sword shooting towards Purple Crow's own sword as it is bearing down on Madame Mu!

Ying Ming rushed to the rescue, yet he had no weapon. He could not use someone else's sword as he did before; he must rely on his bare hands! But how could he stop a killing sword barehanded?

Just as the sword was about to strike, Ying Ming brought up his right hand to block it. Even Purple Crow was astonished, thinking, "This kid is crazy! Does he really think he is a sword? He thinks he can block my blade with his bare hands! I'll cut off his hand!"

Purple Crow rushed forward with increasing speed, when he suddenly realized that Ying Ming's right hand was not reaching for the point of his sword, but rather for the flat of the blade!

The flat side is one of the most vulnerable parts of a blade. It has no attacking power! Reaching for the flat side, even a powerful bare hand was enough to break the attack!

Yes! Ying Ming's hands met the flat of the blade and a loud sound rang out. Purple Crow's blade was forcibly deflected and he fell back two yards!

This defense seemed simple yet any swordsman understands the difficulty and complexity of its movement! A blade moves quicker than the eye. To reach the flat of the blade in that instant requires someone who knows the path of the blade by heart. If there were even a minute fraction of error… then not only would the rescue fail, but the rescuer would also be in danger!

Purple Crow was stunned!

"What? He's only eleven years old, how can his chi be so powerful? He couldn't have practiced for more than eleven years, yet his chi is comparable to a 50-year-old master's. Is he a genius?"

During their struggle, the deflected chi of both parties fell on the powerless Madame Mu, leaving her breathless. Her knees grew weak and her hands loosened. The jade pendant she was clutching flew from her hands towards Purple Crow!

"Ah! The pendant… Ying Ming gave that to me…"

Seeing the pendant flying towards Purple Crow's sword, she lost her composure! Because this pendant was the only gift from Ying Ming! It symbolized his acceptance of her as his mother! The pendant was a link to Hero's birth parents. How could she allow it to be ruined in her moment of carelessness? Madame Mu suddenly rushed forward to catch the pendant before it could fall by Purple Crow!

She couldn't let the pendant be destroyed; she would not be able to live with that knowledge! But she underestimated Purple Crow's ruthlessness. Seeing this woman rush forward towards his range of attack, all for a worthless piece of jade, he laughed and made a decision, just before she caught the pendant…

"Ying Ming, Mother got your pendant back!"

Purple Crow suddenly lifted his sword!

Madame Mu was even closer than before! The sword stabbed down on her chest! There was no one to save her now! Unless someone could stand in front of her and block the sword with his own body...

But what would happen to this person...

"Mother!" Hiro and Ying Ming both screamed. Hiro rushed forward with abandon, hoping to block the sword with his small body. He's giving it everything he's got!

But no one could predict, that Hiro's love would not be greater than Ying Ming's…

Even though Madame Mu was not his real mother, it did not matter.

Between people all that is really needed is a bit of love, selfless love, even if she is not his real mother! But she had cared for him selflessly all these days, even protecting his gift at all costs. An innocent loving woman like that should not die…

Ying Ming reached his mother before Hiro, and then…

He stood in front of Madame Mu and blocked the sword with his body. Purple Crow's sword went through his left shoulder and blood sprayed up. A hero bleeds!

Hot hero's blood was spilled. Did he save Madame Mu?

No! Ying Ming faced her, and he found that although he blocked the sword, his body was too small and Purple Crow's blade much too long!

Too vicious! Too cruel! Too evil!

The sword passed through his back and into Madame Mu's heart and out through her back!

His blood mixed with hers! These two, mother and son, finally shared the same blood. Though they were not born related, they became blood-bonded…

Everyone in the hall stood silent! They stopped! Even the leader of the assassins, Little Dragon King stood mutely watching. He could not believe that Mu Long's adopted son would do so much to save his mother. What did she do that deserved his sacrifice? And the old pendant he gave her, was that worth her life to protect? The confident Hiro stood aside numbly.

Madame Mu clutched the pendant she recovered. Her kind face turned towards the bowed Ying Ming. Blood slowly seeped from her heart and mouth; she was slowly dying, but she still tried to speak to Ying Ming.

"Ying… Ming, no! Hero! Your… jade pendant… I won't let go. Tonight… you did wonderfully, you didn't… disappoint… me. I…

can't... disappoint... you either. I didn't... want to disappoint... your birth mother... My son, I... have done all that I can to be a good... mother to you. Although, I know...I am a kept woman, a mere caged bird, I am not... and never will be worthy... of being a great... mother."

Seeing his mother struggle on her dying breath to tell him this, Ying Ming could not help but say, "No Mother, you have always been a great mother, you are my most honored... mother!"

"Really?" Madame Mu's blood began rushing faster out of her wound, her life fading. With a smile, she continued.

"But... sadly, I am just a... failure...as a mother. Even with my death... I can't make you... lift your head..."

"No!" With Madame Mu's condition getting worse, he knew he could not afford any more delays. Actually, he had planned to grant her wish tonight at the banquet. He was planning to lift his head up and make her happy, but who knew... His small head began to rise up to face her.

"Mother, you are not... a failure! There was a reason why I was planning to keep my head down... for the rest of my life, but...tonight..."

"I will make your wish come true!"

With that, Ying Ming lifted up his head and looked into Madame Mu's eyes.

This is the first time in his life, he directly looked at Madame Mu's matronly face!

This was also the first time, Madame Mu had clearly seen her son's face. Sadly, it would also be the last!

Not only Madame Mu, but also everyone in the hall saw him too! The assassins stood in shock! Chiu Hong was stunned! Xiao Yu was stunned! Mu Long was stunned! Even Hiro stood stunned!

Only Madame Mu smiled, because she felt lucky to have seen, before her death... a hero lifting up his head!

She finally realized why he always kept his head down!

She finally understood his reasons!

Because he was no longer a bowed hero, but...

Just as Hero lifted his head, the clouds over head churned and a storm blew in, as if the heavens themselves were screaming for the hero.

In the small town there was a middle-aged man who was passing through the crowd. He looked up to the star and discovered something.

He mumbled to himself, "A sword legend has come, how could this be? In the thousands of years of history, I have never felt such a powerful sword chi..."

He could feel the sword chi from so far away? The middle-aged man had an ordinary face, but he possessed such extraordinary sensitivity, who was he?

No matter who this man was, he must have had something to do with the way of the "sword," a man of wisdom regarding all things "sword" related.

"Finally, it's coming true! I thought it a mere legend, but today, I feel the sword chi coming from ten miles away--a chi more powerful than Sword Saint. Who can possess such chi? Who is this person?"

"I can't believe that there is a swordsman more powerful than "Sword Saint"! Okay, let me find out who you are!"

With that, the middle-aged man began walking towards Castle Mu. He didn't seem to believe in the legend, but he hoped nonetheless to find it...

A life, the way of the martial artist...
The storms accompany me on this road.
Lonely life, I travel alone.
Through all fear, separation...
Tasting all love, hate...
The lonely sword dances in the leaves
Until the erhu song ends and all have left,

The final regret...
that I alone am fated.

Nameless One year old

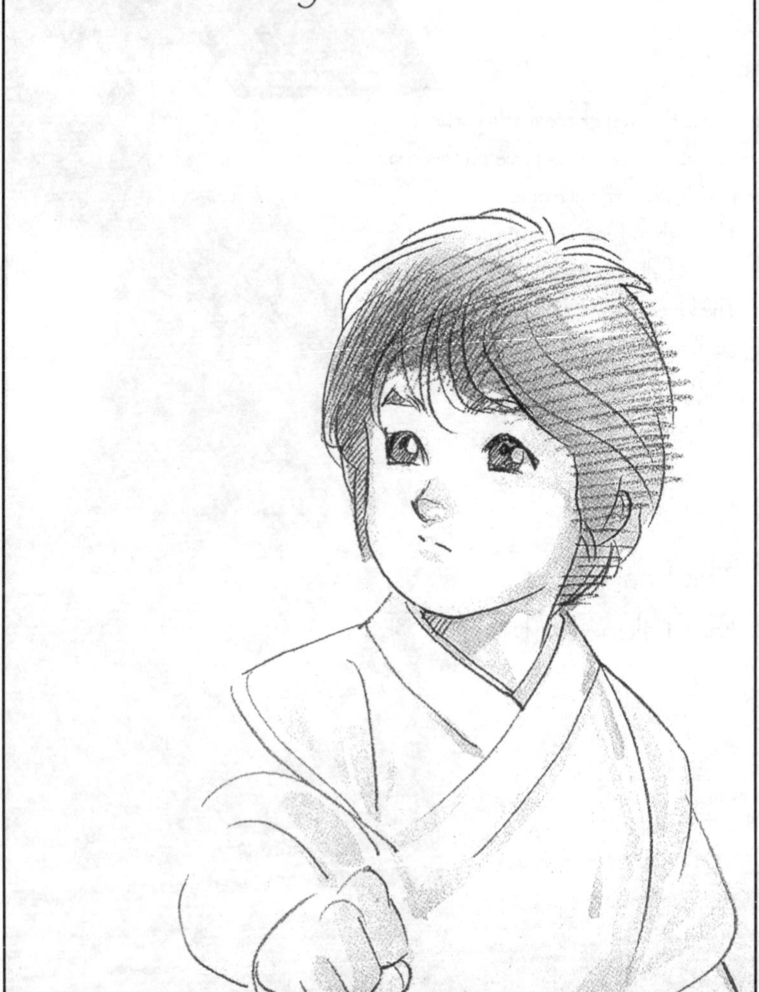

Looking back...

Always outside the door.

He always experiences "love and hate" outside the door! The first thing he really knew of the world, was when "he" was only one...

He just turned one, but he is not like other boys his age, clutching their mother's skirts, protected from all harm. He already knew how to stand on his own two little feet! And he knew how to walk, and how to stand alone outside the door.

He sees how he affects all the adults around him, their life, death, love... hate!

The first time he experienced "life, death, love, and hate" was with his first master, Chong Yang's "love" and "hate!" He was only one, standing outside the door, quietly, unable to help his master Chong Yang, or master's wife...

"Chong Yang! Chong Yang!"

"What is it my wife?"

"Chong Yang! We have no more rice."

"What?"

"Chong Yang, why don't you write to master Mu Long! Seeing that you are his youngest son, Ying Ming's first teacher, and that he is living in our home--Mu Long should send us some money..."

"I don't think... that is such a good idea."

"Why not?"

"My wife, you know there are some things I haven't told you. This boy is merely Master Mu's adopted son, he has been dubbed a lone star, whose bad luck hinders all those close to him. That's why Master Mu doesn't like this boy, and last year he sent the half-year-old boy here to learn martial arts. He was merely trying to give the boy away, and the money he gave us is meant to last for many years. I don't believe he will be sending us any more money."

"What? So… this child is cursed? Why didn't you tell me earlier? No wonder I've been sick since last year. I spent all the money that Master Mu gave us on medicine! Ying Ming has made me sick! Chong Yang, let's send him back to Master Mu!"

"No!"

"Why not!"

"Because this child is special!"

"What's so special about him?"

"My dear, don't you see it? Look at this child. He has the face of a hero. When I went to see him last year, I knew that he would grow up to be a great hero! Also you know he is only a year old today, yet he learned to walk on his own and is already so strong. He has excellent potential to become a top martial artists! I, Chong Yang, have been studying for half my life, but my skills are just average, and there is only so much I can teach. But I have a chance to be this genius-child's master, to build up his foundation; it is the chance of a lifetime!"

"All right Chong Yang! I'll make it simple for you! This child has been with us for half a year. You've been taking care of him day and night, sometimes even forgetting your own welfare. You treat him better than you treat me. I… I've had enough. Now that I know this child is a lone star, I can't let him stay here another moment. I want you to make a decision now, which one of us do you want? Him or me! Who are you going to choose?"

"My dear, don't do this to me. Ying Ming will grow up to be a great swordsman. His childhood is rife with misfortune, and we should not treat him so. When he becomes a hero, we will have a part in helping him get there. Its all worth it… don't you see?"

"Hum! So in the end who are you going to choose? Him or me?"

"I…" Chong Yang hesitated.

In that moment of hesitation, he lost her.

He saw her leave him never to return.

The one-year-old Ying Ming stood outside the door, watching his master's wife depart in anger. Could his young mind understand, that he had already brought unhappiness to his master? His master would rather be abandoned than abandon him?

But Chong Yang turned to look at Ying Ming standing quietly by the door. Chong Yang suddenly felt that this child understood what took place, but maybe he was mistaken.

Forcing a smile, he gently patted Ying Ming's small head, saying, "My child, don't tell me… you understood what just happened? But don't worry, child. It doesn't matter what I sacrifice; I won't leave you. You are a natural warrior. I feel honored with the chance to pave the way for you. Actually your adopted father changed your name to "Ying Ming," but that should not have been done. You should always be called by your original name: "Hero"… Because only Hero can describe your features and the potential I see in you!"

Yes, because he was born with the face of a hero, when his master first laid eyes on this boy, he already knew he would accept the responsibility of being his teacher.

Everything was because of his face, his hero's face...

Ying Ming looked up with his small eyes at his first master Chong Yang's worn face, seeing the forced smile upon his face. Even though he sheds no tears for his wife's departure, his heart was undoubtedly in torment.

True! The one-year-old Ying Ming had not slept that the night. He secretly walked to his master's bedchambers, and heard his master weeping. The young Ying Ming, stood silently outside the door, watching his master's tears, watching his love, hate. The now one-and-a-half-year old boy watched his master without emotion. But when Chong Yang was about to die, he seemed to have heard faintly... The boy finally opened his little mouth, and spoke.

"Master!"

A child's first word. It wasn't Mother or Father; it was "Master." This master must have made a huge impression in this child's young mind, to be the closest and dearest one to him.

He watched for another 180 days, until finally his master passed away! His master died of grief!

The simple word "Master," represented the grateful heart of a student.Chong Yang died happily.

Yes! He never had a chance to teach Ying Ming any martial arts, but for all that he sacrificed, he deserved to be remembered as Ying Ming's first master.

After Chong Yang passed away, Ying Ming was taken away by Mu Long's servants and sent to his second master. Then when Ying Ming was three he stood once again outside the door, looking at his second master within his haunting cycle of "life, love, hate and death!

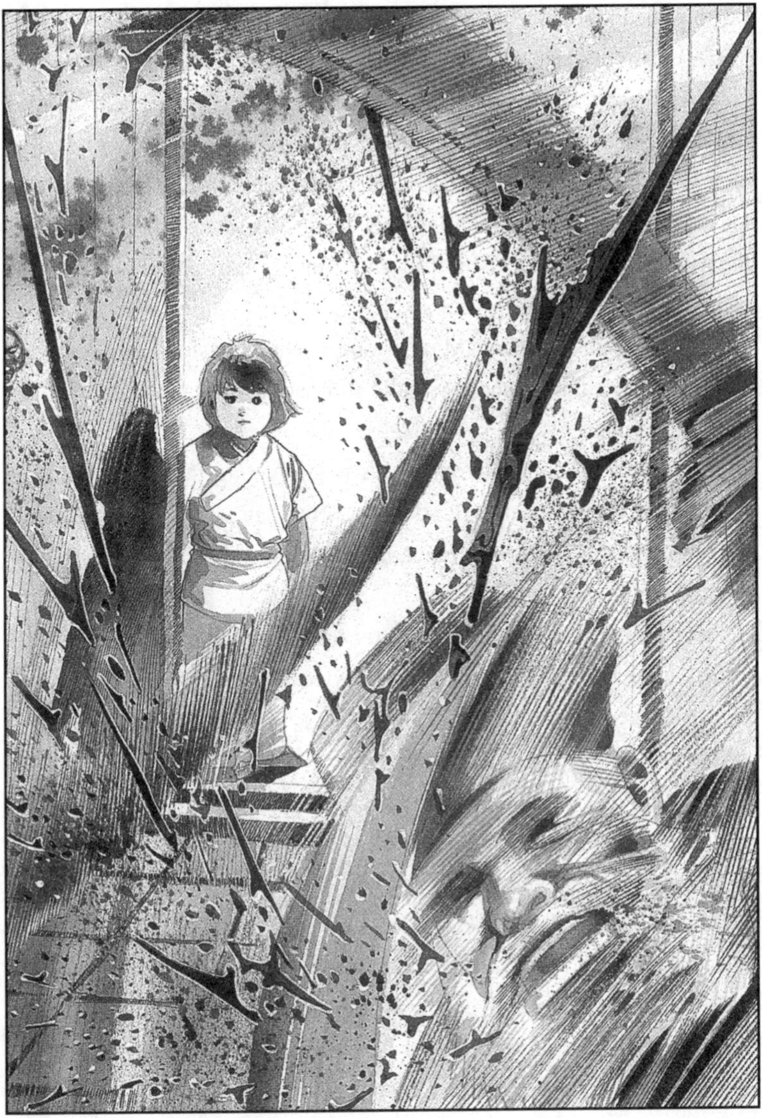

Still outside the door…

His second master treated him with kindness no less than his first master, Chong Yang. But his second master had made too many enemies. And they finally caught up with him. While his second master was skilled enough to escape the onslaught… His enemies changed targets, and began to attack the three year old Ying Ming. To protect this child genius, his second master traded his life and allowed himself to be killed in exchange for Ying Ming's life!

The three-year old Ying Ming, stood silently outside the door once again, watching the master his small heart had just began to honor, being carved in eight!

His master's blood splattered on his tender young face, as the elder's eyes looked towards him in kindness, as if to say he was dying without any regrets! From that moment on, the three-year-old child began to hate his own face!

It was all because his second master loved him so much, that he was willing to sacrifice his life to save him. Because of this face, because of this hero's face!

After that…

There was his 3rd, 4th, 5th, 6th, 7th, and 8th master…

All the masters seemed to come from the same mold. Each was about forty, and in prime condition. None of them should have died so soon. But sadly, each one of them passed after meeting Ying Ming! And each one died without any regret! As if in their short life, dying to help this child, this future legend, made their life worthwhile!

And truthfully, Ying Ming never disappointed any of his masters!

From age five, he began learning chi gong. The masters found him to be naturally gifted and his abilities grew at an astonishing pace. In two years he could fight on par with his 5th master.

At age six, in a mere three days, he mastered his master's entire style and made corrections to improve it.

At age seven, his understanding grew! Upon watching any martial arts style, even once, he could understand its essence. He memorized every kung fu form he had ever seen, and the more he learned, the more he progressed!

Finally even his masters could see no end to his potential. He progressed beyond their wildest expectations and surpassed each of them!

Their abilities were always lower. They could never determine how far he would progress! Also Ying Ming always kept quiet.

When an ordinary hen hatches an eagle, the poor hen will never understand what the small eagle will one day grow to become, with its majesty, its strength, far surpassing its own... The eagle is strong and extraordinary. One day the eagle will take to the skies, full of vigor and energy, but will it remember the hen that raised it?

At a tender age, he could already remember each of his masters' sacrifices. He recalled the lesson he learned repeatedly. His small heart ached with pain. Each of the masters died without regret for his hero's face, though they knew he was a lone star and he would be the death of them. This was the reason, he wouldn't let anyone see his face!

He wouldn't allow anyone to be sacrificed because of his face, or die because of his lone star misfortunes!

A hero, who always keeps his head bowed.

Finally in his 11th year, he decided that he no longer wished to progress further in martial arts.

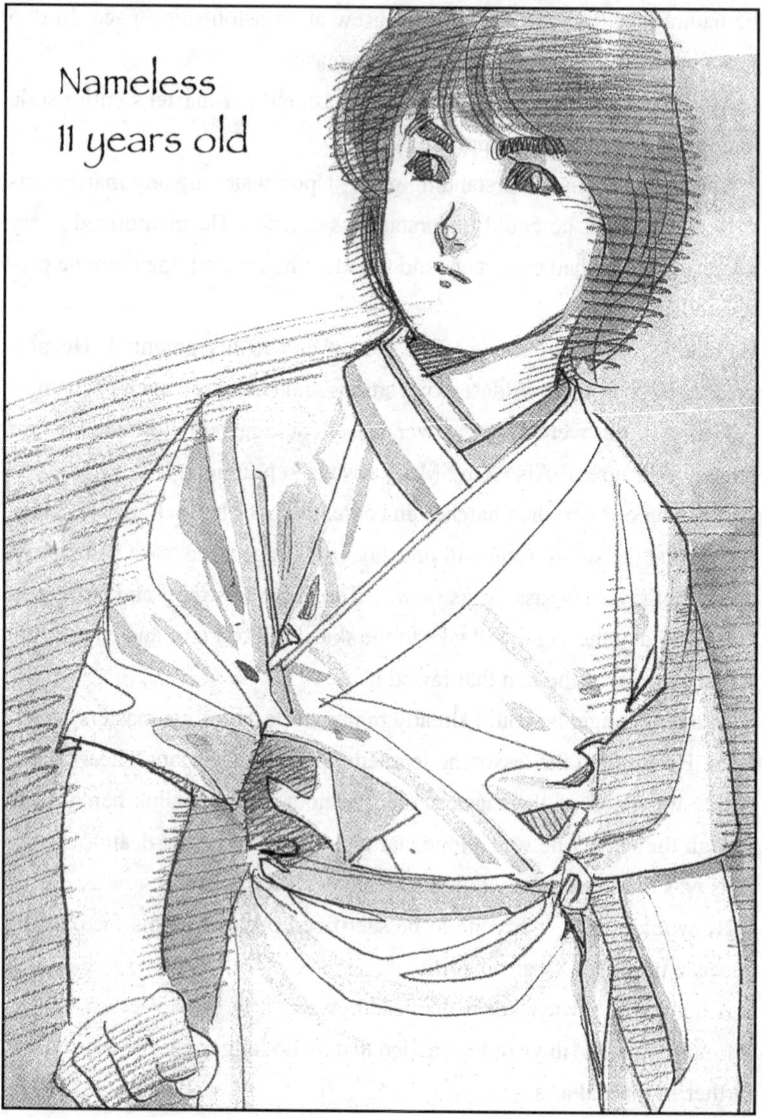
Nameless
11 years old

He wanted to become an ordinary person.

He did not want anyone else to die as a result of his questionable destiny as a hero. But sadly, no matter how he kept his head bowed, how he tried to avoid people, how he would not let anyone see his face, a lone star is always a lone star, and in the end he brought death to the one who had become dearest to him! The only one he really could call family.

Madame Mu!

Tonight, like eight other distant yesterdays--eight other unforgettable funerals for masters who have passed on, his heart filled with sorrow.

Blood poured in rivulets from Madame Mu's heart, flowing along Purple Crow's blade to Ying Ming's shoulder; this sword connected the mother and son pair, but also severed their fate.

The eleven-year-old Ying Ming naively believed that if he just kept his head down so that no one could see his hero face, he wouldn't inadvertently cause the death of others....

To protect the gift of a simple jade pendant, Madame Mu sacrificed everything to protect a promise that she made to him. She rushed towards certain doom. Who could've known that this fragile, admirable woman could think a promise more important than her own life?

His life inevitably revolves around death. If he can't escape fate, then he won't try to any longer! He will lift up his head and let Madame Mu see his face!

This is the last thing that he can do for his mother.

Purple Crow's sword continued to drip blood, as it remained embedded in the bodies of Madame Mu and Ying Ming. In his moment of shock, he forgot to pull out the blade. He could not believe that a young boy would so courageously stand in front of her to block the sword!

All the assassins and guests in the great hall froze in horror, but when Hero lifted his head, the commotion began!

Everyone began talking all at once!

Even Purple Crow seemed to awaken and hurriedly pulled out his blade!

Ying Ming's face was revealed, a hero's face!

They finally understood why Hero always held his head low.

That hero's face, also has…

It has a ray of piercing sword light!

How could a child's mortal face glow with such a light? Upon closer inspection, he found that it was not the boy's face that was glowing, but his eyes!

His eyes shone with a light as sharp as a sword!

The glow danced through his eyes, as if they could at any time come lose and kill all those he glanced at.

A sword is the king of all blades, but in the end it is still a weapon of destruction. When the eyes are like a sword, even a prosaic glance is enough to thwart an enemy's chi! A glance to kill all enemies!

Hiro, who has been dubbed by Sword Saint as the "Ruler of Swords," stood stunned not far from Ying Ming. His eyes also shone with light, always glancing into the hearts of others. But compared with Ying Ming's eyes, his paled!

Both their eyes shone with sword light. Hiro's light was like a sword stabbing through one's heart; but Ying Ming's eyes were not so simple. His eyes would never look into the heart! Instead they seemed to pierce through and break the hearts of others! Everything became dust! Nothing left! There was no heart left to see!

In an instant, after the gathered crowd calmed, the hall returned to dead silence, as if a god had given this child the power to glance and kill all those in the hall!

Xiao Yu realized why her father described Ying Ming's eyes with such detail; they were the immortal eyes of a hero! His eyes shone with a cold light like a sharpened sword, making those in the hall unable to look straight at him. In the past eleven years, as he grew, his eyes sharpened further into a sword, no wonder he always kept his head bowed. It was not an easy thing to meet the eyes of someone with a glance of invincible swords.

Only Madame Mu was not shocked by this child's gaze. Because she was not afraid to die, she was almost…

She's still happy, because Ying Ming was finally willing to lift his head up for her. She spoke weakly, "I am such a fortunate woman… in… this life… I can… see your… face… My… son, your… face…is not at all… ugly. It… is even… somewhat… like… Hiro's. It's… like… you two… really are… brothers. You… are…like…my real…son. You are a hero!"

Her throat filled with blood and it came gushing out. She was not long for the world. Ying Ming and Hiro called out to her.

"Mother!"

The two brothers pushed their entire chi into their mother's body, hoping to prolong her life even a little while longer. Just then a tall figure rushed over like an angry bear. He struck down the already injured Ying Ming, and roared like thunder,

"You bastard, get away from her! Your horrible luck has killed my beloved wife! Is that not enough for you?!"

In his anger, Ying Ming was flung across the room. He hit the far wall by the door, exasperating his condition and the blood splattered across the floor! But no matter how much he hurt, Ying Ming did not make a sound and quickly was on his feet!

This time he did not try to get closer to Madame Mu, because the person who flung him aside was Mu Long!

Now the father and his true-born son pushed their chi desperately into Madame Mu. Although Ying Ming had learned from many teachers, his chi was not nearly as powerful as the top General Mu Long!

He knew that if he weren't around, Castle Mu would probably be better off! He knew that if not for him, Madame Mu might not have died for a simple jade pendant! He knew if he weren't around, Madame Mu might recover under Mu Long's care…

If he didn't exist, then maybe everything would be better!

Everything was because of an unlucky lone star…

But although Mu Long's chi was enough to level mountains, he was not a god. No matter how much he and Hiro tried, they could not save a woman who had been stabbed through the heart. Mu Long had been a great warrior in battle, holding the lives of countless men in his hands. But in the end for all his power their was nothing he could do for his dying wife!

After some time, Madame Mu awakened and opened her eyes with effort. Looking to her husband Mu Long she uttered, "Long, you're…crying?"

Yes, Mu Long was a famed warrior, always so full of authority. Yet no matter how powerful he was, he truly loved his wife with all his heart. Madame Mu was a woman anyone would love. Mu Long's tears brimmed his eyes.

"My… wife, don't… speak anymore. Hiro and I are trying to prolong your life, you… will survive."

Madame Mu listened, but shook her head sadly. Weakly, she looked around to see Ying Ming standing alone by the door.

"Long, why do… you not let…Ying Ming approach?"

Hearing her mention Ying Ming, Mu Long answered with great anger.

"My wife! That god-forsaken bastard… has already done enough to hurt you. Why do you want him to be near you? Just let him be!"

Madame Mu smiled bitterly.

"Long, don't… treat Ying Ming… so cruelly. He is… a really good thoughtful… child. What happened today… with me… it is justice!"

"Justice?" Mu Long exclaimed with shock, even Hiro and Xiao Yu were truly mystified, they couldn't understand why Madame Mu would say such a thing.

"My wife, I… don't understand what you are saying!"

"Long, you think I don't really… know? Ying Ming was not a baby you found. You bought… him."

Hiro, Ying Ming, and Xiao Yu couldn't understand, but Mu Long's face turned ashen-- he knew in his heart. He knew he bought Hero for three taels of silver. In the end, Autumn went crazy with grief, her fate remaining a mystery. As for Hero's father, no one knew where he had gone either.

"My… wife, you... already knew? When did you find out?"

Looking down at the pendant clutched in her hands, Madame Mu spoke quietly.

"A long time ago. I already knew. That year when… you brought Ying

Ming home… and I saw the jade pendant… I knew… Because, that jade pendant, I've seen it before… on Autumn. Then Ying Ming was not yet born. She already… wore this… pendant, with her son's name. She was hoping that her son…would soon… be… born…"

Madame Mu saw her wearing that pendant carved with the name "Hero." That day when she saw Ying Ming with the pendant, she was shocked, and she knew without a doubt that it was Autumn's son, Hero. Later she went in secret to see Autumn, but she found out from the people in town that she disappeared in a storm-filled night! Rumors said that she went crazy when her husband sold away her son, but they did not know to whom. Her husband also disappeared that night.

Knowing these things, Madame Mu kept quiet, she really did not know why Mu Long purchased this boy, until…

Until one day, when she was in Mu Long's study, she found the letter about Sword Saint's challenge, and the deed to Hero for three taels of silver…

She began to understand the magnitude of what her husband had done! He bought a boy to replace his son in battle, splitting apart Autumn's family…

But, although Madame Mu learned the truth, she still did not want to tell Mu Long. The damage had been done, and she could not find Autumn. It couldn't be helped, if she told Mu Long what she knew, in his anger, he might hurt Ying Ming…

So Madame Mu had kept it a secret, although she knew that she owed Autumn, and her son more than that. To help her husband make up for this mistake, and to build some good karma for him, she decided to treat Ying Ming as her own son. Actually, even if she had not known of Ying

Ming's parentage, she would have done the same…

So much has happened, but now the truth is finally revealed! Mu Long face turned pale at his wife's words, yet he showed no sign of remorse.

And Hiro, he just glanced at Ying Ming, he could not predict that his adopted brother would have had such a complex background. He could not believe that Ying Ming was a sacrificial lamb for him!

Ying Ming heard everything, but he didn't react.

Because, he was just a sacrifice? Just a sacrifice? So, his life was so cheaply bought after all.

Madame Mu waved Ying Ming over to her.

"My… son, come over… here…"

Mu Long intervened in anger.

"My wife! Don't let that bastard come closer! He will kill you!"

Madame Mu smiled.

"Long, you know… I'm already dying. So many years… I've always been good to you. Today, I just want you to do… this…one thing…for me, let…Ying Ming… come to… me…"

Hearing his wife's dying wish, Mu Long could not refuse, with anger he stared at Ying Ming and roared.

"Bastard! Crawl over here!"

Hearing that, Ying Ming looked to Madame Mu's loving eyes; he hesitated for a moment, and finally, slowly began walking towards her.

He approached Madame Mu, but stopped several feet in front of her.

Madame Mu was on her last breath.

"Ying… Ming, why… don't…you… come… closer?"

Ying Ming answered with sorrow.

"I… I am a lone star!"

Seeing his uplifted head beginning to bow, she quickly said: "No... My...son! Don't...bow down...your head...again! Don't... ever... bow... down... to... fate! Don't...lose...to fate!...Don't...let it... Change you!"

She is already so close to death, yet she never forgot to encourage her son to live life fully. She truly cared for him. Her hope for him was not lower than Hero's birth mother's hopes for him. After a series of words, her breathing grew ragged. Not wanting to see her suffer further, Ying Ming hurried to lift his head and look towards her.

"Yes..." she said. "lift... your head. That's... right! My... son...don't... ever... believe that you... are some lone star. If you really... believed... those charlatans then you will always be a lone star. My...son, listen...to my... advice. Don't lose to your... fate. You... have to... beat it. You have to take... your life into your own hands. Because... only when you defeat it, will you become what your... birth mother... Autumn hoped you would be... a... hero!"

Madame Mu began coughing violently. Trying to ease her discomfort, Hiro stepped in.

"Mother, you need to rest, or else..."

Madame Mu shook her head.

"No... if I don't speak now, then I... will never have a... chance later. Hiro, there's a... favor mother wants to ask... of you... come closer..."

What was it she wanted him to do? Everyone looked with curiosity, Hiro brought his ear close to Madame Mu's lips, and she spoke softly into her son's ears. No one could hear what she had said, only Hiro. His brows wrinkled, and his expression became uncomfortable.

"Mother is... this really okay?"

Madame Mu smiled.

"Hiro, I know this is not… fair…to you… But your father owes them too much, and this is… my dying… wish… you… you…" Madame Mu looked expectantly at him. This woman had been asking all her life, her husband, and now before her death, her son. For Ying Ming, she had so much to say…

Seeing the anxiety in his mother's eyes, Hiro seemed to have made an important decision. Without regret, he looked towards her and answered with conviction.

"All right! Mother, I will do it!"

What did Madame Mu ask of him? Why was it so difficult for Hiro? When Hiro agreed, Madame Mu's pale face showed happiness, as if a heavy burden had been lifted.

"My son It's all…up to you now… You have to remember my last words… to you… That is you can not hope… to accomplish all. But… answer only to your… conscience!"

Try to accomplish all, but answer to your conscience! Yes, that is the hallmark of Madame Mu's life. Her hallmark for her son "Hero".

Hiro slowly absorbed her words.

"Yes… If I can answer to my conscience... Mother, you've accomplished that in your lifetime. Don't worry! I won't disappoint you. I will strive with all my heart, to do what you ask…"

Madame Mu smiled with satisfaction, because she knew her son; once he's made a promise, would follow through! No matter what it takes!

Madame Mu turned back towards Ying Ming, weakly she lifted up the jade pendant and offered it to him.

"My son, this pendant your mother… can't take it where she is going...

I have to give it... back... to you..."

Ying Ming looked stunned, he couldn't understand why she was unwilling to accept this gift even in death. Madame Mu knew his unspoken question, and explained.

"My son, this is from your birth mother Autumn... This is her last gift to you... I saw her sewing... into the night to...earn enough money to buy... this. Jade can ward away... evil, I'm sure that your mother must want you... to keep this by your... side... She hoped that... it would bring you... peace and health... You can't give it to just anyone... don't forsake her wishes..."

Ying Ming looked at Madame Mu's dying face, and her outstretched hand with the jade pendant; he didn't want to take it back. Looking into her eyes, he said, "You're not just anyone. You are my mother. You, are absolutely worthy of it. If you really don't want it, then I will..."

Ying Ming reached over and took the jade pendant from her hands, with a snap, he broke the pendant in two...

"Ah...Ying... Ming, what... what...are you... doing?"

One half still had the words "Hero" carved on it, the other half with "For my beloved mother,"Ying Ming returned to Madame Mu's hands.

Yes! She is not just anyone! Madame Mu was his mother! She was half his mother, so he gave her half this pendant. He just wanted her to go in peace!

To bring peace to this woman he loved, he was not afraid to break this priceless item! For her peace of mind.

Madame Mu did not want anyone to feel sadness in her passing.When Ying Ming broke the pendant and said "she is not just anyone," Madame Mu held in her tears, but was truly touched. Eventually her tears fell.

Clutching the pendant half with the words "For My beloved Mother," she said, "Thank you my son, you are…so thoughtful. Now… when I am travelling the road to death, I will… always remember the words… carved here… I will remember that I have a son that makes me proud… Hiro... and another son so devoted… A son that in my heart…should be called… Hero. But I could only… be his mother… for such a short time… I wish I… had more time, because I can't wait to see him live his life… with his… head lifted… becoming a hero that everyone looks up to… that day when he becomes…a hero… I want to see the day he takes destiny into… his own hands… that day…"

Madame Mu's eyes began to droop, and her breathing stopped. Her hands continued to clutch the pedant half, as if it were a treasure…

They thought she might be tired from speaking for so long. But looking at her peaceful face, Hiro put his right hand under his mother's nose…

No outburst! No commotion! No crying! Hiro numbly pronounced to Mu Long: "Father, Mother has passed away."

Passed away?

This fragile woman really did not have time to see that troubled boy grow to become a mighty hero.

"Auntie…" Xiao Yu could hold back her tears no longer. Chiu Hong's tears streamed down her face. But Hiro stood by without a single tear… Yet no matter how strong he tried to be, his normally calm hands tightly held onto his mother's face trembling, as if he didn't want to let go…

Answer to your conscience! Answer to your conscience!

Her dying words echoed in Hiro's mind. It filled his entire heart, filling his life…. Will he live his life… answering only to his conscience?

And Ying Ming, what of him?

No one had the time, inclination, or heart to pay him any attention. If they did, they would find that...

"AHHHH!" A scream rang across the great hall, like thunder through the skies! The once famed general Mu Long, rushed to her side and tightly embraced the body of his dead wife. He reared his head up to the heavens.

"Why! Why do you have to take my wife away? Why do you have to treat her thus?"

"I, Mu Long have killed countless times on and off the battlefield. If you have to take someone, strike me down with your lightning! Why do you have to kill my wife? Why my beloved wife? She was a good woman! A woman like her should be praised as a saint! Why did you kill her? Why..."

The guests stared in shock; none could have predicted this strong flood of emotion would flow from the famed general Mu Long!

"Answer me! Answer me!"

Mu Long never treated anyone well, and was thus never popular. Even still he held a treasure, a devoted wife who waited for him at home. When he returned late at night, she would rub the sleep from her eyes to welcome him, would massage his back and comfort him? No matter what wrong he committed, she would always stand by him, kindly supporting him, even sacrificing her own life to right his wrongs...

No one understood their unspoken love for one another. Who could understand the pain he now experienced in losing his wife?

The uncontrollable pain caused Mu Long to scream and cry in sorrow. Suddenly the whole hall shook with the force of his chi, as the guests covered their ears in fear!

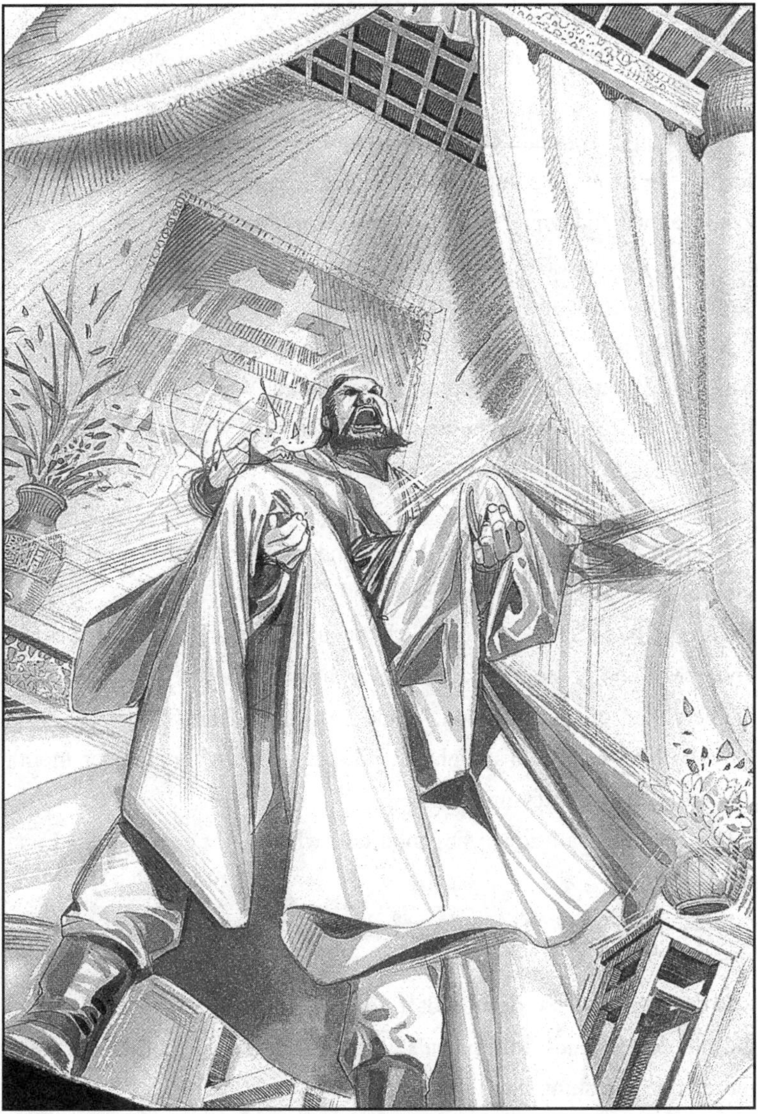

Hiro put his hand on his father's shoulder.

"Father! Calm down! Mother has really died, you can't bring her back…"

How ironic! A young child who should be grieving, was instead comforting the strong and authoritative father? Hearing his son's words, Mu Long calmed and wiped away his tears. Numbly he spoke.

"My… son, you are right! She will never come back! She will never come back! But who caused all this? Who is to blame?"

Mu Long looked at Ying Ming, through his gritted teeth he spat out, "It was... you! You unlucky bastard, you killed her! Your bad luck killed her! It was you! It was you! She was so good to you, why did you kill her? Are you happy now? You must be happy now? You… Get out of here! Get out of here!"

Roaring, Mu Long lifted his left leg and kicked out three times! Three vicious kicks swept towards Ying Ming!

The supposed lone star was able to break eight swords; he could easily dodge Mu Long's three kicks. However, he chose not to…

The sound of cracking bone could be heard! Ying Ming took those kicks with his back held straight. Blood shot out from his shoulder, mouth and nose. His wound worsened!

But he didn't fall down; he stood tall, which only angered Mu Long more.

"Bastard! Why won't you leave? Why won't you leave? Get out! Get out!"

Roaring, Mu Long kicked out a dozen times with full force. The boy did not dodge at all. In moments all the kicks landed and the sound of more bones breaking morbidly echoed out.

His eyes where covered with blood. His mouth was split and his shoulder, legs and ribs were all broken. His face filled with blood, or was it tears?

Why would he take Mu Long's kicks without dodging? Maybe because, he understood his father's pain-- a hurt like no other that he too shared!

But his strength was no match for his father's in the end. Although Mu Long was a palm strike expert, his kicks were still powerful. Ying Ming withstood each kick, except for the final one...

The last kick, he could not bear! Because this kick, had Mu Long's full force and fury!

"Bastard! I want you to leave!"

Ying Ming's body was lifted clear off the ground and shattered against the wall. The wall collapsed behind him, clearly Ying Ming was greatly wounded.

But although he fell, he still slowly, surely, stubbornly stood up. His will astonished all those in the great hall.

But more surprising was a man's scream and a series of ten more... The crowd looked over and saw...

The leader of the assassins, Little Dragon King and his group, kneeling before Ying Ming. In his hands, Little Dragon King held Purple Crow's bleeding head!

Ah!

Everything changed!

The assassins have killed one of their own!

Those who came to kill Mu Long, were now kneeling in front of Ying Ming!

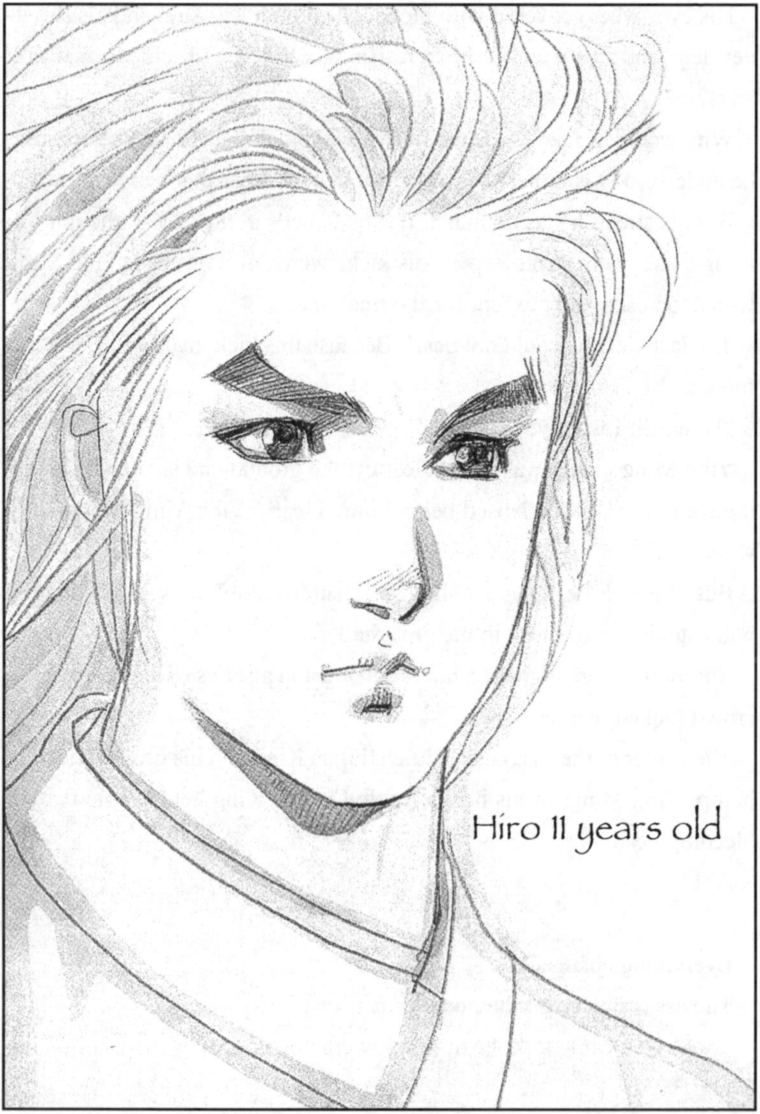
Hiro 11 years old

Little Dragon King, the leader of the assassins, had resumed killing. But the victim is one of his own. Purple Crow's face still showed a look of disbelief that his own leader would kill him!

All the guests could not believe it! But Little Dragon King knelt beside Ying Ming, proving the truth beyond a doubt!

Little Dragon King spoke to Ying Ming, who stood up to so much.

"You are a great man! You should be called "Hero," not "Ying Ming." You are young, but I am sure that when you grow up, you will be a great hero!"

An admiration showed from Little Dragon King's eyes.

Seeing Little Dragon King praise this son, Mu Long was outraged.

"Damn you! You've killed my wife, and now you're helping him? Have you no shame, kneeling before him?"

"Ha! Mu Long, you dog!" Little Dragon King refuted, "Who do you think you are? How dare you treat me with such disrespect? I am warning you! My vengeance has not ended. One day I will come back for your head to avenge my father! Today I killed Purple Crow, because he did not keep his promise!"

With that Little Dragon King ripped off his black mask to reveal a brave, loyal visage. A man of about 26 or 27, but he had the mien of a great veteran warrior.

Turning his face toward Ying Ming, he said, "Brother Ying Ming! I have always been a man of honor! Today we came to assassinate Mu Long. We've made a blood pact to kill him alone. No matter what, we will kill him and harm no one else, especially women and children. Purple Crow betrayed this pact, dishonoring us by killing your mother…"

Little Dragon King's voice grew deep, "Your mother, Madame Mu--we've witnessed how she tried to save your pendant. She's a good woman, worthy of our respect! I killed Purple Crow to pay back the life he took! A life for a life!"

An honorable man! But a man like him, why would he kneel in front of this small boy?

"Brother Ying Ming, although I have killed Purple Crow. Your mother is still dead. Our assassination mission has caused this. I accept full responsibility! Brother Ying Ming, will you become my sworn brother?"

Before he could answer Little Dragon King and his band began kow-towing to Ying Ming. The sound of their heads hitting the ground rang through the hall.

The sudden turn of events shocked Hiro and Xiao Yu. Even Mu Long felt overwhelmed; he was not as decisive as Little Dragon King. Only Ying Ming... He stood tall like some revered statue not yet fully completed, unmoving... Perhaps because he had no more strength to respond. After suffering Mu Long's kicks, he should not be able to stand. But he did not want to break the promise he made to Madame Mu. He knew that if he fell down or fainted, Mu Long would leave him, he would never make it to Madame Mu's funeral.

But Little Dragon King misunderstood his silence, he thought Ying Ming was still angered over his mother's death. Little Dragon King always spoke his mind.

"Brother Ying Ming! I know that you are saddened over the death of your mother; perhaps now is not a good time. I know that killing Purple Crow and bowing is not enough to atone for my sins. How about this? I offer myself as your willing servant."

What? Servant?

Little Dragon King looked to be of noble stock. He ruled over his own compliment of warriors. He would be willing to serve a small boy? Looks like this Little Dragon King was no ordinary person either!

Little Dragon King continued, "I know this is quite sudden! But seeing you deflect those eight swords at such a young age, you have such incredible bearing. I know that you will grow up to be a great man! Your mother's hope for you is not ill-placed! I feel the same way. I know that one day you will be a great hero! Brother Ying Ming, if you don't mind, then please be my master. There is only one thing I will not do for you. I must kill Mu Long to avenge my dead father. Other than that, you only have to command, and we will obey!"

Gaining such a loyal, honorable man as a servant was really wonderful. Little Dragon King lifted his head and looked expectantly at Ying Ming, but Ying Ming merely stood without any sign of emotion. After a long moment, he finally spoke.

"I don't want to be a servant to anyone. So I don't need anyone to be my servant!"

The simple words are answer enough!

"Don't want… to be a servant to another, so you… don't need anyone to be your servant?" Little Dragon King slowly savored the answer and the admiration in his eyes increased.

"Good answer! Good answer! You don't want to be anyone's servant, so you don't need anyone to be your servant. I can see that you are a just man! There are too many people in this world that wish to lord over others, yet you can maintain a sense of justice. No, I, Little Dragon King, am completely won over!"

With that, Little Dragon King bowed deeply to Ying Ming once again,

"Brother Ying Ming! If you don't want me to be your servant, I won't force you today! But In my heart, you are already my master! If ever you should need me, just call for me, and I will come with my brother, we swear with our lives!"

Finishing his pledge, Little Dragon King and his band stood up, and turning to face Mu Long, Little Dragon King spit out,

"Mu Long, you dog! I really envy you! Though you've been such a corrupt official, and you've wrongly murdered my father, you have the luck to marry such a wonderful wife, you even have a great adopted son! In fact…" He glanced towards Hiro, "Even your true-born looks to be quite a character! The gods are really unfair! My father was a just official all his life, but your slander at court cost him his life and all my family's lives. I was the only one who escaped the massacre. Fortunately, I have become the leader of a clan. You better be careful! I will let you go today, because of Madame Mu's death. But one day, I vow that you will pay with blood! Let's go!"

Little Dragon King's band quickly gathered together and leapt out the Castle. Little Dragon King walked to Ying Ming and bowed one last time.

"Good bye young master…"

Before the words faded, he was already gone, disappearing into the night.

Mu Long was planning to chase after Little Dragon King, but holding his dead wife in his arms, with his pain so fresh, he decided to forego it. Besides Little Dragon King vowed to return, he can finish him off then. There is still one more thing he must attend to now…

Looking towards Ying Ming struggling to stand, he yelled, "Bastard! I told you to leave! Why don't you go? If you don't leave, I will kill you now!"

Mu Long put down his wife and started towards Ying Ming.

Ying Ming continued to stand his ground. With his level of injury, he wouldn't be able to move if he wanted to. But he stood resolutely, if Mu Long was intent on making him leave, there was little he could do but die!

The normally taciturn Hiro suddenly called out.

"Father! He, can't leave!"

Mu Long stopped in his tracks, turned back towards his son, and asked, "Hiro! This cursed child has killed your mother! How can you still help him? Why can't he leave?"

Hiro's bright eyes fell on Ying Ming's face, and he gave a most unexpected answer.

"Father, I don't want him to leave; it's not because I want to help him! It's because ... I hate him!"

Hearing his son's words, Mu Long stood shocked. Xiao Yu was even more shocked. She knew that Hiro barely spoke two words to Ying Ming, what hate could there be between them?

Not waiting for the crowd to speak, Hiro coldly said, "Bastard! Who do you think you are? Do you think everyone is here to make you king? I, Hiro, won't abide by it!"

"Did you know, from the first moment I saw you, I already hated you? You're so pathetic, you're not worthy of being my brother! I spit on you!"

Hiro's attitude towards Ying Ming changed drastically. Everyone was filled with curiosity! Although Ying Ming stood mutely to the side, he seemed to be a little shocked as well.

"But I know that mother loved you so, I didn't want to make her sad, so I always pretended to help you! Before she died, you know what she told me? She said that we owe your family too much. She pleaded with her dying breath for me to take care of you. I don't want her to die without peace, so I pretended to agree! But don't dare think I will carry this out! Now mother has died, and my promised died with her! I don't need to pretend to be good to you to please her! From now on, I will use every method at my disposal to torture you!"

Xiao Yu listened with shock. She could not image that her cousin Hiro was so deep. His temper so great. She looked towards Ying Ming, and saw him stifling the pain of his injuries. Although he tried to keep calm, his face grew paler with each word.

Seeing Ying Ming's face, Hiro seemed to grow bored of the game. He pouted and added even more cruelly,

"Do you know why I want to torture you? Because you are really useless! You are like a pile of dirt, you are... Cheap!"

"My mother treated you with such kindness, but you would never lift up your head! She died protecting that pathetic, old, cheap jade pendant! My mother should not have died for that! Bastard! It is you who killed her! It's your jade pendant that killed her!" Hiro's gaze fell upon the jade pendant clutched in Madame Mu's palms. His eyes seemed to shoot out angry flames.

With hatred he said, "It's this unlucky jade pendant that killed her! It doesn't deserve to be in her hands! I'll get rid of it!"

Quickly, Hiro took the half piece out of Madame Mu's hands, the silent Ying Ming finally spoke up.

"No! Don't!"

His breathing was heavy and ragged. But his injured body was still swift!

With his remaining strength, he dove towards Hiro!

Because that pendant half was for Madame Mu! He knew that if she were looking down from heaven, she would be happy to know that it was buried with her. But why doesn't Hiro understand his mother's heart? Why has he done this?

Like a flash of lightning, Ying Ming rushed towards Hiro, trying to grab the pendant piece out of Hiro's hands. Hiro was surprised that Ying Ming still had any energy left at all. In his eyes, a moment of admiration passed, but was quickly covered by the look of hatred. That hatred. Is it real? Or is it a show?

No matter what, Hiro's martial arts was on par with Ying Ming's, and Ying Ming had already sustained so many injuries. Hiro merely suffered a few minor wounds in his fight with the assassins.

Although Ying Ming reached Hiro's hand in time, he didn't have the strength. Instead, Hiro's hand grabbed Ying Ming!

With a wicked smile, he said: "Forget it! Do you think you can stop me? Do you think you are stronger than I am? Bastard! Get out of here!"

With a loud thud, Hiro kicked Ying Ming aside. Ying Ming's body flew through the doors of the great hall, crashed to the ground and rolled several feet.

At the same time, Hiro took the pendant from Madame Mu's cold hands, though she still clutched the pendant tightly. As Hiro took the pendant, he could feel the importance that his mother placed on it, and his heart shook. But in the end, he coldly, cruelly, ripped the pendant from her hands...

"This is the unlucky pendant!" he screamed. "It killed my mother! We don't need this evil thing! My mother doesn't need to be buried with this!"

With that Hiro suddenly flung the pendant…

Ying Ming screamed, "NO!"

"No! Brother Hiro! You can't do that," Xiao Yu also exclaimed, "Aunt won't be able to rest in peace!"

But the two of them, one barely able to stand, the other with no martial arts ability, could only watch Hiro toss the pendant far outside the castle grounds, where it could not be found.

With the pendant gone, Hiro's face lit up happily. He gave Ying Ming another look and said, "What? Bastard! I threw away your pendant, so what? What are you going to do to me? Even if you get better, what could you do?"

Ying Ming looked solemnly at him.

"If you do this, Mother won't rest in peace…"

"Really?" Hiro smiled coldly, "But I don't think so! The pendant is gone forever now! If you can find it, then I'll let you put it back into her hands." With that he turned towards his father Mu Long.

"Father, have you ever seen such a pathetic bastard? Seeing his pitiful face makes me so happy! Why don't we leave him here? I want to continue torturing him, to avenge my mother's death!"

Seeing Ying Ming's face filled with sorrow, his heart chilled slightly, but his anger dissipated somewhat.

"Hiro, my son, you are right! You have made your father happy! Let's let him stay here, we'll see what happens to him! Hehe…"

With that Ying Ming continued his stay at Castle Mu, but he changed. He no longer kept his head bowed.

Now, no matter how much hurt he suffered, he still stood up straight and tall. He kept his head up, perhaps because he made a promise to Madame Mu never to bow down again...

A woman who sacrificed her life for the pendant.

He won't let her down.

Never again will he bow down.

Though Ying Ming never bowed down, he remained as aloof as before. The same night that Madame Mu died, late into the night, rain poured down like tears from heaven. The heavens seemed to be lamenting for the death of a good person. How could that kind woman not live to see the day her son became a hero...

The grand Castle Mu turned into a silent tomb after her death.

In the pouring rain, there was someone who was still not sleeping. With severe injuries and crippling heartache, he braved the pouring rain. Outside in a vast bamboo forest beyond the walls of Castle Mu, he searched the wet undergrowth...

He is Ying Ming.

No one treated his injuries, no one tended his wounds and even he himself forgot about them. There is only one thing on his mind; that was to find the other half of the jade pendant!

The heart-felt wish he gave to Madame Mu.

Mu Long and Hiro have long retired for the night, although they might not be able to sleep so easily. Ying Ming, no matter how much he hurt, rested only briefly, and then despite the pain, continued searching through the bamboo trees. The heavens seemed especially cruel, with such a heavy downpour...

His body was soaked through already, and the rainwater broke through his wounds that had briefly sealed. Blood began dripping from his wounds, but he didn't care; he just wanted to find it... As long as he found that jade pendant, Hiro promise would remain, and he would put the pendant back into his mother's hands...

But the forest was huge, and the ground had already been turned into a churning mud pond. A heavily injured person crawling on the ground looking for half a pendant, was like looking for a needle in a haystack... Ying Ming searched for a long, long time, but to no avail. He didn't give up, but no matter how hard he pushed himself, he was still only human...

Rain, not only soaked through his clothing, but also made him shiver with cold. When his teeth began to chatter, the rain suddenly stopped...

...or so it seemed to Ying Ming. Generously, someone had covered the boy with an umbrella, risking everything to block the rain for a hero...

It's Xiao Yu!

Ying Ming lifted his head slightly. He was stunned. He couldn't believe she was out in the wet dark night... for him.

"It's... you?"

Xiao Yu's hair was quickly soaked and stuck to her delicate forehead. Raindrops beaded on her face. It was difficult to tell if she was crying for the hero. She nodded.

"Cousin, Ying Ming. Just let it go. It's so small, and this forest is so big. It's probably already buried by the rain and mud. You won't be able to find it"

"No!" Ying Ming insisted. "I don't believe it. If there's a will, there's a way. If it's here, I will find it!"

Turning, he began searching once again.

She was deeply touched to see him searching, so desperately in the cold

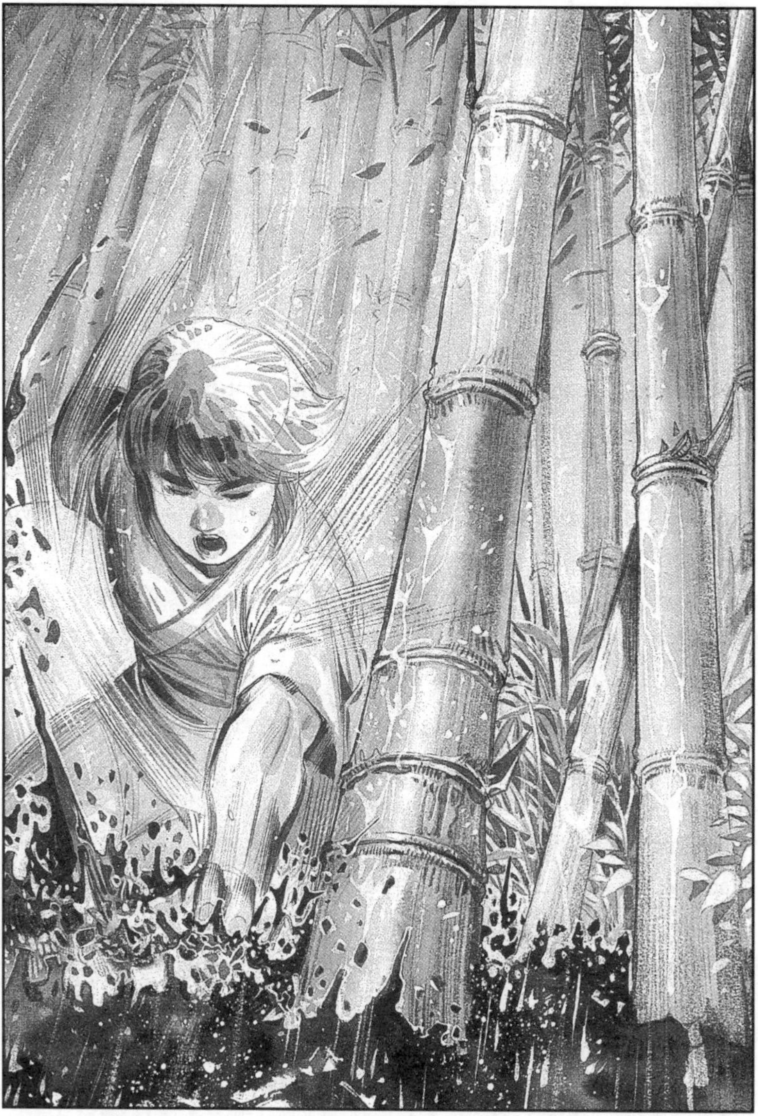

rain for the pendant he gave to Madame Mu. Clenching her teeth, as if she's made some important decision, she tossed the umbrella aside and began digging through the mud!

She did it for him! She did it for him!

Ying Ming's brows creased in concern.

"What are you… doing?"

Xiao Yu found herself getting cold and her teeth began to chatter, but she continued for him. She forced a smile on her face.

"I'm… looking for the jade pendant!"

Ying Ming looked at her, and saw her innocent face, coldly he said, "I… don't know you that well. You don't need to help a cursed person like me. You're just a weak girl; go back and rest in your room!"

Xiao Yu stopped, hearing her kind concerns being so carelessly tossed aside.

"Cursed? Cousin Ying Ming, do you still think you are a lone star?"

"I've always been!" Ying Ming cut in, "And I not only killed my birth mother, but I also killed Madame Mu… I agreed never to bow down again for her, but…"

He paused and looked into her eyes.

"I also don't want to get close to anyone. I don't want to see anyone!"

His meaning was clear. Although he would no longer bow down, Madame Mu's death taught him a important lesson. He was indeed an unlucky lone star. Although before her death, Madame Mu repeatedly asked him to not bow down to fate, he felt that he could not escape it…

Hearing his words, Xiao Yu's heart ached. She didn't want this brave, heroic boy's heart to grow so weary. Also she discovered that when Ying Ming spoke, his eyes no longer had that sword like glance as he did at the banquet…

The sword, has already died in his heart… He is now no longer a hero. Without any light, he was merely a mortal who had lost to his fate.

Xiao Yu felt regret for him. The hero had become a rusted sword. But she still wanted to admire his dedication to find the jade pendant for Madame Mu, so she said, "Very well. Brother Ying Ming, since you don't know me that well, and you don't need my help, I won't help you. But I think that auntie in heaven would want you to find that jade pendant. I am looking for that pendant for her… not you! Are you satisfied now?"

Not waiting to hear an answer, Xiao Yu knelt on the muddy ground and renewed her search.

Silently watching Xiao Yu's delicate figure and her hands digging through the filthy mud, Ying Ming's lip twitched slightly.

It was a smile of gratitude.

But Xiao Yu is concentrating on her search, and she did not see his small smile…

And he didn't need her to know.

He didn't want her to get close to him.

But some people will always be drawn together, as if there were a special force pulling them towards one another. Although they were merely eleven, after a long, long time, he would find that he would never escape her.

He could not escape her love.

The rain fell not only on Xiao Yu and Ying Ming, it also fell on some-one else, standing in a dark corner of the forest, watching Ying Ming and Xiao Yu as they search for the jade pendant.

The same rain had soaked through his body. His carefully combed hair in disarray, stabbing into his eyes and onto his handsome face. But he did not seem downtrodden. His face reflected his gratitude as he looked at Ying Ming intently searching through the mud.

He was grateful that his mother did not die for nothing! His mother had a son that could make her truly happy!

Hiro didn't go back to bed, why was he standing here in the rain? Why is he here?

Not only was he soaking wet, but also his expensive white robes were covered with dirt. His fingers were raw and bloody, but why? Why are his robes dirty? Was it because...

He gave up his comfortable bed in the castle, and dug with his bare hands looking for an item? Until his fingers bled?

What was he digging for? Did he find it?

He's already found it!

Although the task seemed impossible, he made the impossible possible! He found the needle in the haystack!

In his bloody hands, he held a small item, a jade pendant inscribed with four small words, "For My Beloved Mother" carved in to it!

Huh?

How did he find it before Ying Ming? If he threw it away, why did he go searching for it? Was it because he didn't want Ying Ming to find it and put it back into Madame Mu's hands?

Hiro's dirty hands and clothes showed that he had been digging for some time. He found the pendant before Ying Ming, perhaps because he was not as hurt as Ying Ming. But now, he was even more alone than the supposed Lone Star. His robes were too white, he was a child born with privilege--a son of a rich, noble family. When his white robes were soiled, it seemed even more regrettable.

But Hiro didn't seem to mind it. He didn't care about his haggard appearance, as he clutched the pendant tightly in his hands, silently watching Ying Ming and Xiao Yu.

"Answer only to your conscience… Mother, if you are watching from heaven, do you see it?"

"I don't need anyone's acknowledgement, and I don't need 'him' to know what I am doing. Mother I just want you to know…"

"That aside from an adopted son who will become a hero, you also have another son who will fulfill your dying wish I will live as you've taught me… I will answer only to my conscience!"

A lonely and sorrow filled litany, as if chanting for a long lost mother… But Hiro did not shed a single tear.

He tossed the pendant towards where Ying Ming and Xiao Yu were digging.

A figured garbed in a dirty white robe vanished from the forest like a lonely ghost. Vanished in the pouring rain. It was he! A lonely ghost!

Although Ying Ming led a difficult life, no matter what, he still had Xiao Yu by his side, helping him.

But Hiro had no one. No one would ever know. Ever after, he would do the things his conscience beckoned…

Not long after Hiro left, a joyous exclamation filled the forest! It was Ying Ming! He finally found it!

"Cousin… Ying Ming! You found it… the jade pendant? You found it? That's great!" Eyeing the pendant in Ying Ming's hands and hearing his happy voice, tears rolled from her eyes.

It's great! It's great! But if Ying Ming looked closer at that half pendant, he would find that the jade was stained with small, almost indiscernible patches of blood, the blood from a kind boy's fingers…

The blood stains on the pendant tell a touching story, a story of an older brother helping his adopted brother find a precious item and digging through the dirt until his fingers bled…

But the wind was too strong and Ying Ming happiness too great. Ying Ming did not see the story of the blood stained pendant. And the blood was washed away with the rain…

Like all life, death, love and hate, it washes away with the passage of time.

The next day, when Hiro visited his mother's temporary resting hall, he put in his prayer incense, and found that in her hands, she held once again that halved jade pendant. Ying Ming had also already put in the first of the prayer incense.

Seeing Hiro, Ying Ming quickly shied away, as if in shame.

"Big… brother, I've found the pendant. Please keep your promise."

He hoped that Hiro would keep his promise and allow Madame Mu to be buried with the pendant.

"Really?" Hiro answered coldly. He glanced at the pendant in Madame Mu's hands and then glanced back at Ying Ming.

"You sure are capable! Don't worry, I keep my promises!" He hid it all so well.

To make his mother's dying wish come true, he will act it out.

Ying Ming's eyes shone gratefully.

With anger, Hiro continued, "But don't be happy just yet! If you continue to stay here, I will make your life miserable!"

Without another glance to Ying Ming, Hiro turned back to his mother's alter and hurried to put in his prayer incense, as if Ying Ming's were merely a useless pile of garbage. With his back turned to Ying Ming, and incense burning, a hot teardrop fell on Madame Mu's resting face.

A hot teardrop...

Whose tear is it?

Perhaps it was an 11-year-old boy, who had held the tear in for so long after his mother's death, a tear of no regret...

But Ying Ming did not know, because the teardrop flowed along Madame Mu's face into her eyes, as if she was the one crying.

For a son that she was proud of...

A tear of gratitude.

At the same moment the tear fell upon Madame Mu's kind visage, in a darkened corner of Castle Mu, a pair of eyes stared through the Castle walls, directly at Ying Ming and Hiro.

Those eyes were filled with curiosity, admiration, and inquiry.

He's finally found them. He's finally found two who could become legends.

The eyes seem filled with wisdom. A pair of eyes that could see through everything related to the "sword."

A pair of "sword" eyes!

End of Volume 1

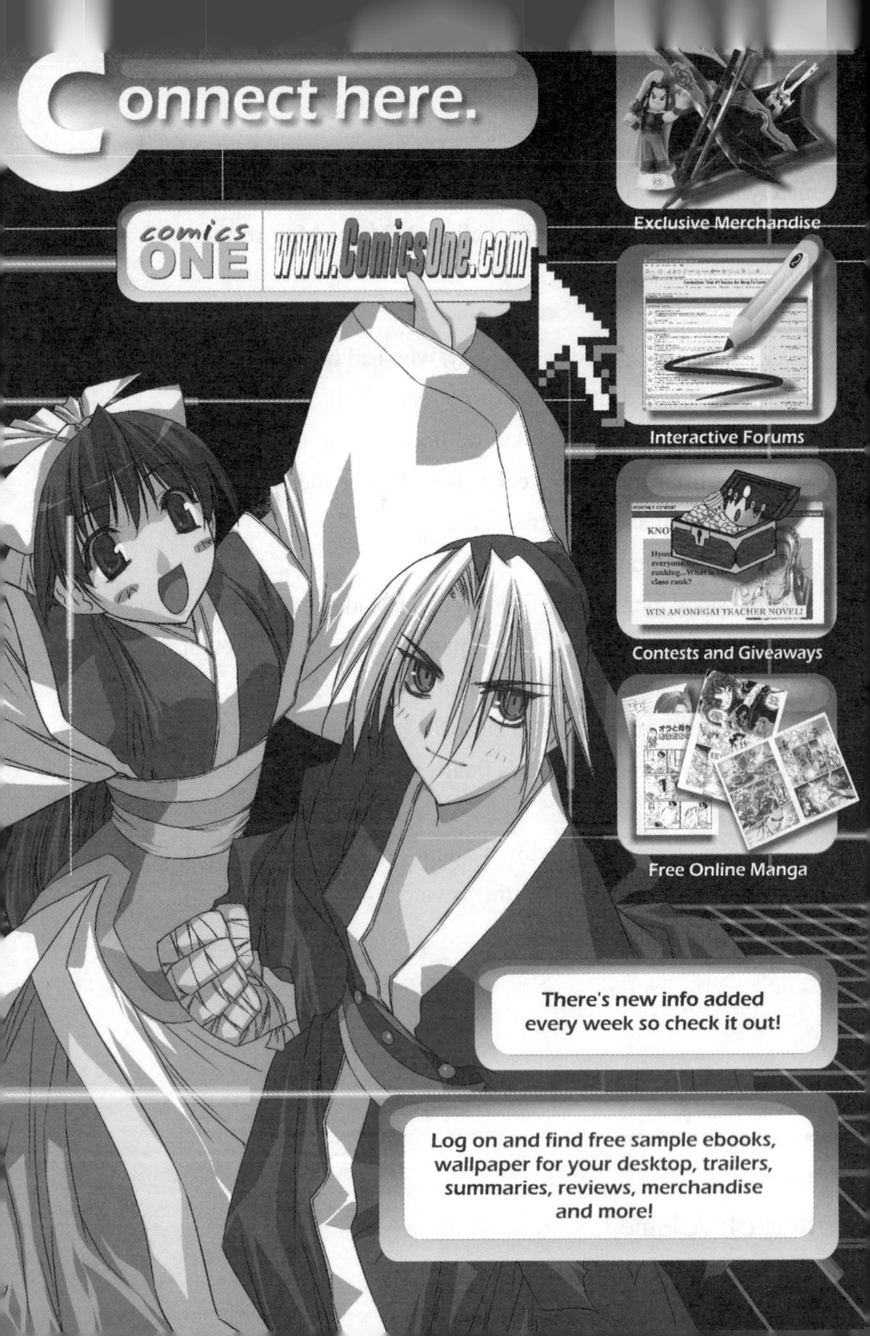

Connect here.
comics ONE
www.ComicsOne.com
Exclusive Merchandise
Interactive Forums
WIN AN ONEGAI TEACHER NOVEL!
Contests and Giveaways
Free Online Manga
There's new info added every week so check it out!
Log on and find free sample ebooks, wallpaper for your desktop, trailers, summaries, reviews, merchandise and more!